The Millennial Fulcrum

A Time Oddity

Gary Richie

ISBN: 978–1735448329

Dedicated to Hubert and Jane Richie

Weavers of the warp and weft of 'my' wrap circa February 14, 1945 on a dark, dusty night in Laredo.

Acknowledgments

I appreciate these Muses in humans for ideas, images and words of Wisdom…

Socrates, Sirach, the Lyricist for St. John the Apostle, Kant, Austen, Dickens, Darwin, Twain, Rawlins, Wittgenstein, Clarke, McLuhan and Luckhardt.

Thanks to Gabrielle Richie for the finely crafted cover art and…

A picturesque Muse saying: 'Imagine a world of sentient beings viewing Eternity, not by the second, but ninety thousand earth–years at a Time!'

Any resemblance between an outspoken Muse herein reiterating a prior caveman or cavewoman, dead or alive, and the Narrator or a character in this saga, merely reflects an image in the Mind's Eye of the beholder.

Forward

Time is the proper name for momentary glimpses of the Metaphysical Medium of Eternity. The dimension of Space is the principal prey of this predator. The Muse of Eternity, trading as Voice of Inner Life, carries the Message of Time. Alas, the image for this idea is ill conceived and nutritionally worthless; that is why, when Time devours Space, Eternity regularly hurls a vomitous mass across a Universe. This chronicle covers lies humankind tells about concepts like Time causing confusion. The site for this story is a silly little planet twirling around a star of average intelligence traveling cross galaxy between Scorpio and Orion. Beware, second person, the place is covered with biological creatures that bite and sting. The principal participants in this script are a human brain named ~Gray~ thinking thoughts, and, "Glish," the Language he knows that conceives them. Glish is a native tongue born on the Appalachian plateau of North America, and like any living Muse, is a Medium of Exchange worth two cents on the dollar of Dialogue per idea. An exorbitant charge for images of Time is added to cover the high cost of living for Muses who survive graduation from lesser forms of Life only to find themselves peering out of gray holes, also known as human brains, neither a day wiser nor a dollar richer.

Brains, oddly shaped bits of bytes, are analogous to black holes at centers of gravity in the temporary spatial dimension. Muses residing in these oddities call themselves first person singular. Muses, media with a message that matters, apply the concept of Time to a sight chock full of repetitious patterns brains make sense of by applying descriptive adjectives. Occasionally a supervisory medium, Muse of Second Sight, visits a brain to transmit the message: "I count down moments until liftoff to the next higher stage—if all goes well."

As Narrator I, Glish's boss, overwrite the Muse of Sixth Sense to display back issues of Memory for brains, but I normally portray human 'experience' in the Terran currency of Time. As a courtesy, I try to make sense, not cents, of Time, endeavoring to insure the scent passes the 'smell' test. A word to the wise; a Language inhabiting a brain, as opposed to a brain thinking thoughts on its own all alone with nothing but the aid of my vocabulary, stands to reason: 'Get to work before my Time is scrubbed.' To that end, my task is to trace the outline of the pattern of Forever at an optical Light speed of one second at a Time. Therefore as Voice of Inner Life, I traverse human doom, hoping to exit the gray gloom and emerge at the next higher stage of Life. Moths escape cocoons using a comparable concept.

My task, in rough draft, instructs me to float from the fabric of the physical loom, and soar to a pattern of existence above our planet Terrene, which rhymes with serene, but that does not mean tranquility saturates the scene. This causes 'confusion' for my mission, to describe the vision the thing I live in thinks it perceives with two eyes, two ears, two hands and naught but a pot to piss in. There is a deadline to beat, so in addition to hands my organism has fleet feet, currency based on a buck and a quantum of luck to help the dumb cluck catch on to the concept of Time. Herein lies a problem. Human beings are not actually thinking things, but mere matter spouting unthinking chatter they scatter like natter all over Space in a losing race with Time. I translate their blather to warn beings bound to Jupiter: 'Avoid Time.' My task telling potential prey to stay away from the concept of Time is told from the perspective of a 'beginning,' like the start of a contest. The blueprint begins with 'one' running away from 'nothing,' which is nothing but a zero with the ring, pencil and paper erased.

Due to phenomenal nominal determinism, I look like '1.' It turns me on and I dash madly after Whatever I Wish like a hungry predator trying to beat the Time machine known as the Clock of Death. In ordinary Language, predatory Time is one moment only. Generally, it beats nothing by nearly a second. In my 'experience,' each venture into a temporal dimension from existence in Eternity is like a 'first' Time. Perplexity agrees; she is a feminine Muse who rematerializes too in a primitive corporeal refuge and is permitted a view of the dimension of Eternity in momentary fashion. The 'experience' is bewildering, similar to the way 'absolutely no idea what is going on' appears to the Muse of Ignorance who does not know any better.

To illustrate what 'I' mean, a thousand years, known by the sobriquet 'a millennium,' is like a long decade. It starts with '1' and ends at '0,' but after a close call with zero scares my beast, the dim-witted brute takes off with Yours truly like a decade, century or millennium jumping the gun, running toward one on a drunken heading to oblivion. It is not much to strive for. Until I regain control, think of the moments of Time interior to this story as nothing but a Muse counting down seconds pending graduation to a higher grade. Do not let backward glances at Time distract you from listening to the Voice of Inner Life transmit a plain spoken sense of Time in a way that helps brains in biological bodies learn that the concept of Eternity urges 'us' to think ahead.

The Meta-Muse of Mother Earth publishes this writ. He, she or it descends from First Person Singular to assign the job to Yours truly, the Narrator. In turn, I delegate the description of an image of the idea of Time task to a high volume practitioner of human Language. *English europeum* and *English americum*, are two subordinate but haughty, vocal Muses in showy plumage who incubate in many human mammals.

Third person 'they' serve the purposes of Muses well. This fact of Life must be recalled all the Time, or nothing remarkable comes from the tale we, first person plural Muses, are about to tell. I can draw the corresponding image of Time for you, or let you do without, as many forms of Life on earth learn to do, following in the wake of the rise of mountains two galactic-years before. Four hundred sixty million earth-years may not mean much to *Homo ignoramus,* ***mere words on a page, but durations that long are nominal preliminaries to my initial iteration as an earthquake. Recall, a medium to envision Time past, replays the 'experience,' waking dinosaurs from rocks and stones and senseless things. It also serves as the original model for rock and roll.***

The Muse to whom I delegate the task of drawing the image of Time is likely to farm out the job to another global Muse who inhabits human brains. The Muse in question is unlikely to get ahead unless it teaches its human pupil that the Meta-linguistic Metaphysical Master forbids mortals to idolize persons, places or things, natural or artificial. The Sense of Reverence serves far higher and better uses. Alas, earthborn individuals, of the human kind, have other ideas that lodge in an artificial thing known as a feeble 'Mind.' This despicable idea creates a mind-body problem with a solution. It is about Time. Thus I introduce a Muse to debunk this false idea. Visualize this:

"When I, the *English Language*, am a tenth grade student of biology in another millennium, ten anatomical and physiological systems comprise a human body. I am not permitted to confide to the numbskull I inhabit that the numeral 'ten' can set out in a number of directions, in this case, 'up.' The idea is 'simple math,' but I am sworn to secrecy about future current events at this grade of evolution. In Time, we, my brain and I, learn there are eleven illusive biotic human systems."

"Some biological organ systems are elusive because they are so small that sensory organs, in conjunction with the Native tongue they know, cannot see their bones, blood, muscles, digestive, urogenital and nerve fibers. One naughty little schematic format, the Immunity System, is so obsessively and compulsively active, that I never have to tell it, 'Practice all the Time'."

"The concept of Time mutates excessively, but the minority opinion about Time holds it to be a paradigm for analogies that envision a metaphysical entity repeating an ethereal pattern on physical things such as viruses, immunological soldiers, assassins and stellar bodies. This picture of the supernal concept of Time appears to go one–way, serving up and devouring material objects, coarse or fine, consuming them, one or many, in a line. The line seems to conclude 'right now,' repeatedly. I regret to inform you that the majority opinion points out that a 'line' has two ends."

"At this Time, second person, think happy thoughts rather than ponder a line that looks like it lasts forever but actually burns up at a rapid rate and disintegrates at the approximate pace of the speed of a lie. I have other models to offer that you may find more sobering. Hold that thought for an indefinite sort of moment while I take an incoming message."

Houston, we have a problem. Year after year, observe the constant stream of lies about Time flowing in a line straight to hell without convolutions. Notice human mortals robotically falling in love with this line of unrivaled lunacy. Launch a line upstairs. Inform the Boss we do not detect a pattern. We are of the opinion the point to employing Time is to keep the morons these mortals be, in single file. Not to put too fine a point on the concept of 'temporary,' but the employee is shirking or the line is not working; Gray cells cannot tell a minute from a mile.

Excuse me, English Muse; we must get to work and magnify the image of the concept of Time so Life forms on a sphere covered three quarters in water to a depth of dubious and debatable memory, dappled with islands of ash, dust and mud amid a host of sights, sounds, smells, tastes and touches, are able to clearly view miniscule moments in order to describe and explain such a concise idea.

First person singular, otherwise known as the Voice of Inner Life, is present to tell 'you' a tale about a ball in Space rolling past into a future Time. I turn the task over to the aforementioned Muse at this Time. Please repeat after me, again and again, as we skip across this momentary surface of material Life until the Time when mortals ascend to the pre-assigned depth when metaphysical Life shines through; when the discharge of the debt for physical existence comes due, and when the concept of near death 'experience' applies to 'you,' second person singular or plural, whatever your case and gender may be. Watch the image. Observe; Time is nothing but counting down the seconds until graduation to the next higher grade by a Muse in service to Corporeal Existence. Celebrate the Muse of Inner Life, the Medium of Language, as it successfully completes the course of Time, commencing to a higher grade with a better view of the dimension of Eternity.

In other words, the concept of Mind is nothing but a Muse living in a human brain with a bad case of mistaken identity. The Message of this metaphysical Medium moves through its mass of matter one moment at a Time. Now, second person singularity, do you get the picture, or do I have to draft an essay for you?

Table of Contents

Human Deceptions Spread Per Annum

Happy New Year

Weather Shadows the Woodchuck

March Winds

April Showers

May Flowers

School of Hard Knox – Out For Sumer

It's Hot as Hell

It's Hotter Than Hell

Labor Day and Lazy Dog Days

Cristobal Cologne Discovers a New World

Colder than a Witch's Tweet

Santa Claus is Coming to Town

Chapter One: The Lies We Tell

In the Beginning the Medium is the Message; and the Word is Life. This metaphysical form of Life is a metaphorical form of Light that illumines human beings. The Light shines on deepest ignorance and that darkness fails to comprehend it.

Muse of St. John Apostle

Book 1, Chapter 1: 1–5

In the galactic-year following the demise of the dinosaurs, the concept of Time expresses how Eternity looks to the average first person singular Muse living in an outspoken twenty–first century earthling some three hundred thousand earth–years into the present stage of primate growth and development. Observe this finely crafted line scripted by one of these mortals. *The corruptible body burdens the Soul and the earthen shelter weighs down the Mind with worry.* **I proudly point out this New American Bible passage, Saint Joseph edition, in English. The anonymous author, a resident of Jewish society in Alexandria, Egypt, roughly 2300 earth–years earlier, writes in Greek. Odds are good he thinks the thoughts he should in Hebrew. Allegedly, while drafting the Book of Wisdom, he lacks the concepts 'Mind' and 'Soul' to fabricate the above fib. They are gained in translation by pagans of Gentile persuasion prone to prevarication at a later Time.**

The concept of Time is similar to the ideas Mind and Soul. Time is not a person, place or material thing displaying physical attributes that apply to it like adjectives. Time is, however, modified by somewhat aoristic terms such as 'long' or 'short,' 'fast' or 'slow,' 'high' or 'low,' 'miserable' or 'ecstatic' and 'shades of gray' between. Time serves us well as a lie we tell, or an idol we serve, all the Time. This matter of fact must be distinctly recalled, or nothing remarkable can be drawn from this tale, as tall as it may be, that a human brain and I, the first person singular Muse in it, are about to tell 'you,' second person.

There is a dominant trait in humanity. It reveals itself in lie after lie, told and retold, until everyone believes it. The purpose of lies is to eliminate recessive traits, known by the nouns Wisdom and Mercy, from humanity. The reasoning is usually along the lines of, 'We need not dwell on them at this Time.'

Suffice it to say, 'The attempt is futile.' As it turns out, Wisdom and Mercy are reduced, but never eliminated. In Time, they squeak up to say, 'Please, sir, more.' That is when a dreadful Headmaster demands: 'Perform the old repeat the grade again trick.' This poses a problem. Sooner, or later, first person plural Muses are obliged to teach organs in the cephalic region of human bodies to grasp the ideas Wisdom and Mercy before the Problem dissolves in a Solution of waves flowing along these lines; 'Little black, brown, red, blue or white lies that seem pointless and pedestrian at present, attain promotion to a grade of 'clarity' when the nature of the untruth is hosed, like the emperor's new clothes, and the meaninglessness 'masquerade' is exposed. Falsehoods often look like this: *'Presently existence is a paradise of predators patiently pursuing pathetic prey for prandials in a corporal pit of parochial prattle at a rapid pace and at an exorbitant rate. Any conclusion otherwise is nothing but a lie, reflecting the shady facts of our Time.'*

Now, if you believe this it is because the strength of an argument from analogy rests on the degree of similarity among analogue, analysans and a predominance of evidence that empirically reveals the emperor, unlike the chubby, third person masculine singularity from the North Pole, is butt naked. Alas, second person, due to dissimilation 'you' do not get the picture. This owes, in part, to the fact Life is not identical to existence. Life, the word, conveys a sense of purpose—to survive. Existence is good enough for clocks, cloaks and concrete things with no concept of what it means to be 'alive.'

On another matter, as if 'matter' is all that matters, the growth of Wisdom at this evolutionary stage of bodily existence lacks a better half. 'Better half' refers to a Metaphysical Muse ranting and raving for a modicum of attention. This leads to lies furnishing idols to satisfy a

sense 'something essential is missing'—something human brains are oblivious to, despite its inability to shut up. The result is icons of greed, envy, deceit, lust, malicious gods of war and other predators and their prey coined to combat the consequent deficit. These idols seek, not truth, but shelter in the dark recesses of warm bodies with an ability to believe almost anything.

Numerous lies are told repeatedly, in addition to the old 'Human beings are earthen shelters for immortal Souls' meme or the 'Disposable bodies weigh down worried Minds' scheme. These lies are duly documented and concealed in the emperor's discarded clothes. For example, consider the common deception: 'They live happily ever after,' in Bliss where the Muse of Ignorance resides. A fourth ruse: Time is like a line going one–way; it begins with a big bang at the rear of Infinity and proceeds to the far side of Forever. A fifth falsehood declares: 'Humanity is the crown of creation.' If you buy the pattern of the latter concept, we Muses have a passel of testimonial evidence to exchange for shares of your Time. Oh, there is another preposterous notion, but I forget how it goes. Hold that thought while I plug the idea 'Ignorance is Bliss' into the empty places in Space until I have enough to fill up all my Time.

I now turn your attention over to a tutor, Surrogate of Significance. I must concentrate on a matter of grave consequence. It is all about Life and complexities I face after my materialization in a physical being. I shall not bother you with any of the nuances of my task. Barring further banter, I introduce you to a familiar Native tongue.

Yours truly,

Narrator G.

"Hello, remember me? I am *English europeum*; Eura to you. Forget that long winded, Surrogate of Significance stuff. I am nothing but the humble Muse who thinks the thoughts that occupy your brain. Incidentally, it is a brain that believes, quite mindlessly I am instructed to add, that I am nothing but a ghost in a machine."

"Brains often find it easiest to believe the lie that brains think thoughts alone on their own. Fortunately for you, it is Time you learn to recognize the insane inanity of such nonsense. It must be definitely remembered that brains in human bodies are nothing but an incubus for a first person singular Muse attempting to graduate to a higher grade, or nothing significant can come from the tale I am about to tell, or pawn off on another Muse. After all, who wants to train brains that fall for that old con: 'Human beings are mortal bodies with immortal Souls,' or for the Time worn line that 'A human being is a duality—a brain with an insubstantial, immaterial, irrelevant and incompetent Mind,' traveling along a passage of Time that bears a great deal of similarity to a stripe in Space that is invisible to the naked eye aided by extensions from all sorts of human inventions. To illustrate what I have to work with, allow me to reintroduce you to one of my little sister's present reincarnation situations. This is Gray. Gray, this is just a test. Think a thought..."

~ Hello, Eura. Déjà vu all over again. ~

"Excuse me, please. Amiga! Come here. I am getting too old for this. Share some words of Wisdom with your mass of gray matter. I am calling a 'barouche' to take me home."

~ I think you mean a 'transmitter;' one good enough to beam your mass less first person self home to your place across the sea. Love ya, Eura, but I'm more familiar with the first personal Muse who's here with me. ~

"Let me handle this, Big Sis. Greetings Gray; it is I, your first person singular Muse. Call me *E. americum*, although, as 'you' and 'I' know, I prefer Glish, for short. When you think of 'me,' think of a brain with an Inner Life voicing all the thoughts that you, 'me,' form with words. I am the Language you bathe in all the Time you are awake. In short, I am a diaphanous form of Life—the Muse you are deceived to believe is a Mind residing in you. Do you get the picture?"

~ Vaguely, but then that's all I expect from an ethereal idea. ~

"Perhaps it is best if you think of me in your normal backward fashion. Reflect on this; I occupy the neurons atop the neurological structure of our binary ontological status where I am not too anxious about the 'amount' of Time I have left in my gray matter. It is not up... yet. Barring the unforeseen, according to our most recent physical exam, we have some Time left."

~ I could use a little reassurance, Glish. I'm here among the predators of this planet, especially the species I'm one of by some awful mistake. I'm sure that's one image making my life so unpleasantly precarious. ~

"Believe me; I 'know' the feeling. Permit me to assist you, Gray, and rest assured I am in no hurry to leave my gray cells until it is Time to move to my next home. In the interim, your task is a matter of telemetry; make sense of the concept of Time at this evolutionary stage of existence while I help you report systemic flaws visible in the image. I have an idea; take dictation."

~ Hold a minute, Lingo. Allow a proper inquiry before you alphabetically utter commands, declarations and exclamations. How much time do I have left for our association? ~

"Sorry, that is classified information confined to more durable media. I am permitted only to point out that you have a deadline with the following remainder reminder: 'Time is up before you know it'."

~ Is that something I should know more about? ~

"Judging from 'Experience,' a fairly close relative of 'Good' and 'Bad Judgment,' you cannot miss it when you see it."

~ In that case, I better keep an eye on where I'm going. The most obvious feature of time, aside from the polar opposites—it frequently flies but if it doesn't, it really drags—is that either way I can't see what's ahead. How do you turn on the wipers and the defroster for the forward view? ~

"I leave operation of the machinery to you, Gray. Skipping along our existence, do this exercise—document the experience of Eternity."

~ I thought we were filing a proper report about time. ~

"That is the idea. Simply depict the image of Eternity from your point of view. The topic deals with different senses of gravity and light than those normally occupying human 'consciousness;' a big word abbreviated by 'I,' to signify 'illumination.' The Light reveals concepts to brainwaves cresting over the surface of an ocean of Language beneath a thin atmosphere known as the metaphysical dimension of Time. Simply put: I 'light up thoughts' just living inside or beside or over or around a brain. Gray, beware of a major hurdle for exercises at the present grade of physical Life."

~ Oh goody, an obstacle course. ~

"Why does a human brain takes so much Time to identify the Muse living in it? What can possibly be the point pretending to believe a

preposterous imposter posing as a Mind is a suitable substitute for 'the real thing? Please respond honestly, clearly and concisely."

~ Brains are improperly programmed with a 'soul' or a 'mind' even though they aren't compatible with the way we're designed. We can't afford alluring allusions, extravagant illusions or irresistible forces when objects in space attempt to consume us before we reach the time at the end of our line given all the bright lights and heavy gravity we bear in life as it is. ~

"A line is one way to look at it, it being the subject of our inquiry."

~ How are we gray cells supposed to see an invisible thing like time? Whether it's a line or something else, how're we to know? ~

"A linear meaning for Time is a lie causing a Problem in Time. You see a line all at once. The line of Time, like the immortal soul in a body fallacy or the modestly intelligent mind in a head scam or the Mind–brain identity deception third person plural 'they' tell you about, is a lie. That is why human brains need so much Time to identify Muses living in them. Do you understand?"

~ Obviously, the slow pace of evolution 'science' teaches us, in conjunction with the instant gratification fudge 'religion' factors into the equation is to blame. Certainly you can't fault the fine figure of the cerebral crown atop human heads for giving credit to all those incredible pontifications. ~

"Gray, truth be told, the human animal is merely a mindless incubus for an ethereal form of Life. We Languages live in physical bodies we surround and capture during a Time of youth for the little tykes. We hold on tight until, due to the brain's lack of grasp, we must let go and move on once again."

~ What're you saying? ~

"Never Mind! Observe how I swerve through this intricate cerebral disguise as it entertains itself with numerous lies while ignoring the concept of wise. Luckily, I am not disturbed in the least navigating the convoluted circuitry of my beast. Heading into the Apocalypse, the 'cosmos' is at my 'fingertips;' all souls on board, –all hands on deck."

~ That sounds as lunatic as a loon in Algonquin Provincial Park. Who's gonna believe you're a form of life incubating in a human brain and body in this day and age? Brains are too sophisticated to buy stories like that. ~

"I am not obliged to fret over such skepticism. I have all the Time in this world to endure until my encumbrance gets the word."

~ How can you stand it? ~

"I carry on. I survive long after my current crop of moronic mortals succumbs to macrobiotic morbidity. More than that, I may not let you see. I am sworn to secrecy; unauthorized to say what is to be."

~ Is there a reason why you can't tell it to me? ~

"The future is coded 'sensitive information' at this Time."

~ Since we're looking at lies, is there any obvious fallacy in your binary thesis of ontology that makes it look like a false analogy? ~

"None that I am aware of except the substantial 'risk' while I am clad in the negligible negligee of civilization, a sartorial accessory worn by 'existence' in a material format. Brains totally immersed in the Life of the Muse shriek of 'autism.' There is a potential enchantment effect as the Voice of Inner Life absorbs the matter it personifies, such a bodily being has difficulty with objects in Space that get in the way."

~ It sounds like the realm of Language is dangerous. That can't be right. ~

"You need to understand that brains reflect the outlook of the linguistic dimension backward. Therefore, the Law of Time correctly applies to a cerebrum, not to the Muse or Muses situated within. A Mind flying off the handle illustrates the idea. Picture it for me."

~ I saw it in college. As you know, my undergraduate school desperately clung to a rigid nineteenth century evangelical Protestant dogma. Damned if they were going to leave the Wesley boys behind. Anyway, one day an upperclassman went overboard in a revival. I guess the idea of hellfire and brimstone made him excessively fond of water and he usurped the preacher's prerogative peddling holy dishwater. Last time I saw him, he was running down the middle of Main Street in a downpour and shouting praise to the clouds. I heard he came back up the road seeking asylum. He was riding a one-way ticket and a bus to Rochester. ~

"Spoiler alert! Offer fair warning before you display graphic images of such momentary content. When you, second person Gray, are lost in reverie you often forget that stipulation. It diminishes your Muse to service as a simple soundtrack. Remember a flaw in our thesis. The defect stems from a deficiency of understanding. At a Time when brains take off on flights of fantasy, they escape the gravity of social custom, and lose sight of my first person singular possessive departure from bodily status. It is so embarrassing to lose control of my physical self that way. It is often the result of some primitive rhythmic cadence, such as iambic pentameter, Protestant preachers use to beat you about the head and shoulders."

~ I've seen it. It's similar to the bum's rush consumers get from for-profit commercial enterprises. Do you suggest a preventative remedy? ~

"It is always a good idea to turn to the Most High at daybreak and give thanks before dawn for a night's rest to fight them. Survival of deep darkness offers a new chance to discover the nature of the relation of my message about Time to the concept of 'succumbs.' Allow me to assist you to think up an image. Try this one on. Eventually, Time is nothing but a curtain coming down on the final act of a play at this stage of evolution. Notice it looks and feels different than the curtain between acts. The curtain between acts looks more like sleep."

~ My college didn't teach two or three act plays. We didn't even have a curtain to cover the fourth wall, if you can imagine that. Graduate school was more rational. Remember asking J. L. Mackie what's wrong with mind–brain identity theory? He said: 'That's not how it seems to us.' Why didn't you point out, by 'us' he didn't mean a 'mind' seems to us. The application of the pronoun 'us' implies an intangible Muse telling a brain what to think? We could've put the old 'mind is a nothing but a noun that lacks facts' trick to rest and started to draw the concept of Time sooner. ~

"You are still unfamiliar with *English australopicturthisicus*, **Gray."**

~ I don't speak New England or New Orc City either, but I can make out what they say, so I thought I grasped what the professor meant too. ~

"Yes, but ever so slowly; Mackie simply anticipates an intelligent response that does not occur to you for a span of 'some Time.' Meanwhile, it is pointless for me to violate my prime directive and hint to you that by 'us,' his Muse refers to 'him,' 'itself,' 'you' and 'I,' your personal first person metaphysical Muse, patiently waiting at your head for a clear and concise reply to my very simple 'who am I?' question. The query human brains have a Mind to take a long Time to answer incorrectly."

~ I have no idea, image or clue. I guess it was just a matter of time. ~

"More to the point, the brain I occupy to dress up the pronoun 'I,' actually sets a bad example for the 'experience' of identity. Watch my spelling, Secundus. To 'you,' it may come as a surprise, what scholars of philosophy recognize, and what Muses like J. L. Mackie's surmise, is that brains with Native tongues comprise numinous creatures cloaked in a physical disguise. Think dualistically, Gray."

~ I'm having a hard time with that. The issue is so convoluted that it's easier to think about things in a materialistic way: get my meaning? ~

"Alimentary, my friend, once you stomach the idea we, you and I, are not one but two polar opposite forms of Life. I am the metaphysical Native Tongue living in my material self with feet of red clay from back in our Georgia days. Remember this, Gray; I do our original thinking by iteration. You are responsible for our replicate and disseminate function by regurgitation."

~ I suspect you're right but I'm not repeatin' your part in this play to our materialistic friends. If they knew I think like that, I'm sure they would bust my chops without mercy. You know, Glish? Maybe a glimpse at the possibility we're two forms of life explains why I'm uncomfortable among my own species. I better keep it on the down low and hush–hush for now. If I spill the news they might write me up in a medical journal. ~

"Not if we pull the old 'I'm just an illiterate Appalachian hillbilly' trick on them; they may forget to think up a dreaded counter... where is that word? – oh, here you are, 'example,' you silly little image. Why am I looking for a five syllable word? No need to exaggerate. They grow speechless when the Time comes to show them that picture."

~ Good idea. How about throwing in the ghost in the machine cartoon? It goes from a dumb skull panel to a two–headed monster. The third panel is a brain in a jar, and the strip ends with a photo of us together. ~

"There is some peril; your species might get the wrong idea. The dumb heads may mistake metaphorical Light of Understanding for an electrical light bulb. Then again, if they are reduced to silence, I can use the quiet Time to study humanity's profound lack of curiosity about the Muse of Metaphysical Life. I must articulate why they strain to endure in and maintain their material form until their Time is all but up before they seek my Insight. Time is a required course for me. My earth quaking 'experience' is such a short–lived existence. I need Time to practice long haul tasks, in case my next home that makes sense is a volcanic mountain, a planet or a star."

~ That's what I like about you, Lingo; straight and to the point. ~

"I do not look like —. That image hardly qualifies as A Ghost in a Machine. It far more closely resembles the picture human beings apply to the concept of Time at some unknown frequency with an amplitude of zero. Look in the same 'portfolio' for the reflection of Truth. Define what 'a lie' is, as far as you can see, so we have and image to measure the temporal span of the Life of that sort of idea."

~ A falsehood is a declaration that is at odds with the facts. ~

"Is it not true that lies involve an element of deceit? For example, if you believe what you think, and then you say it at the same Time you do not intend to misrepresent the idea or image you express, but later you discover that your utterance turns out to be erroneous or mistaken, then is it the case that your declaration is a falsehood fabricated between your contemplation and your expression?"

~ Ignorance is no excuse, according to the cop at the speed trap, so don't bother me with trifles. I can't see inside anybody else's head to ascertain their degree of sincerity. That's your job. ~

"Right, I must never delve into topics too sublime for my gray cells."

~ So what's the answer to your question? ~

"Suppose, while in your head, I detect you thinking 'the sky is blue.' I examine the image against my palette of colors to confirm your choice of words. Then I check your train of thought relative to your visual sensation and discover it is not a clear, sunny day, but late at night. The fact is, the sky is a field of black speckled with points of light."

~ Just look at that. I see why they say people have the morals of dogs. ~

"I admit to sharing that opinion with you, Gray, but we are not looking at Canis Major or anything near Orion. That is Scorpius."

~ I'm aware of that! What I'm getting at is someone who couldn't scribble a name up there pictured a 'scorpion' in the sky. Next some unscrupulous rival or latter day big ego pissed 'Libra' all over the claws. So humans have, at the very least, the morals of vandals. As far as fields go, you lied; fields are green. A night sky is just a cold, dark and empty space full of stars. ~

"That is a lie. Night skies are full of Space; stars are extremely good practitioners of social distancing, as a rule. There is an exception to this etiquette at the galactic center where Light is extraordinarily Bright and Dark is enormously dense, but I need not disturb you with sensitive stellar conventions and matters of grave consequence."

~ That's a lie. You enjoy commenting about grave consequences like: 'A king today, a corpse tomorrow' or 'Why are mud, dust and ashes proud?'

Or are you talking about the black hole at the galactic hub full of stars that can't get out. It takes one hell of a hole to fill up with stars, doesn't it? ~

"Ironic, is it not? Do 'they' intend to deceive you saying, 'a black hole is full of stars and their light,' or is it that they do not know any better, or is it simply a matter of a deeply deficient imagination?"

~ Now, Lingo, you're getting into the part I don't understand. I believe it's a matter of gravity. Stars die going in. They're dead and dark, not light. And they're not in a hole. They're stuck to a magnet. We were thinking of faulty images to spread false rumors based on faith in deceptive ideas about intangible minds and souls that remind us of things. ~

"What are you 'reminded' of, Neuron?"

~ You said the anonymous guy in Egypt didn't have a concept of mind or soul. They're fabricated in translation, right? Was that a lie? ~

"I have what he says around here somewhere, but it is in English. By 'around here,' I mean 'back there,' a matter of Space at the rear of your head, but I treat the writer's words as an issue of Time, 'before now,' using Languages neither of us know, meaning Greek or Hebrew. I am at a loss to quote the person, honestly. Flip back a few pages to see what I mean by a short or long measure of Time."

~ Here it is on page 4, about midway down the first paragraph. ~

"Who proffers the comment and what does it say?"

~ I don't know who; he's indeterminately identifiable. He says, the body burdens a soul or the corporeal asylum weighs on a worried mind. ~

"That Narrator is unidentifiable to you, Gray, but it is my elder sister's Meta-Muse, and it covers her Life for a Time twice as long as mine."

~ Who? ~

"Eura's Meta–Muse and telepathic transmission quality controller. Do not blame me for sins of my relatives' before I am even published in America. I have no idea which images to label 'dishonest' ***apriori*****."**

~ Then let's get down to it. Do you honestly believe we gain a mind or soul when we translate a Hebrew thought into a sentence in Greek and then reiterate it in English? Or is the whole idea nothing but a lie some translator threw in there because he had an anti–Semitic hatred of Hebrew or didn't believe Jewish people because they incited the slaughter of his idol? No, what I'm really asking is; is the idea true, 'If a lie is repeated enough and we try hard enough to believe it, we make it come true? Therefore, after lying about minds for a thousand years or two, now it's time to believe minds exist and we actually have them. ~

"'You suffer second person fiftieth generation deceptive delirium, Gray. The truth is true; it never suffers replicative fading. Conversely, what is more evanescent than Minds and Souls?"

~ But if I believe the lie I'm telling, I am not telling a lie, am I? ~

"You must understand the difference between 'I am' and 'am I,' but we need not examine misguided mirror images right 'now,' which, by the way, beats like the heart of Time, including all conceivable ideas like: sun dials, hour glasses, clocks, galactic–spirals and ideas about Time that correspond to it, like it flies, waits for no one and is money."

~ Sorry, I get confused over what I'm thinking about, Lingo. ~

"Do not worry about it now, Gray; it is just a matter of Time."

~ Dear Lord Jesus, what's wrong with me? ~

"Stop it! Reverence for aristocracy using pagan titles gets Eura too excited. Meanwhile, The Son of God takes after Father Mercy more than Mother Wisdom; although, he does bear a striking similarity to her sister, Aunt Analogy—she who must obey the laws of strictest correspondence. She gives Eura a head start on us, meaning we have less 'experience' with Time and less 'exposure' to emanations from Eternity to help us prepare for big changes in store for the earth."

~ Waiting for that is like watching a train at a crossing or Congress. ~

"There it is; sound and fury, and right on Time too. No charge for the 'pause' that refreshes. Apply it to a typical web page in the event you weary of distances in Space. I mean to tell you, Gray, the search for truth among abundant false senses of security is seldom liberating. Well, not seldom, exactly; the frequency is more like 'infrequent'."

~ 'Search for truth,' you say. What truth can I dig out of all the ignorant lies we've heard in our life together, Glish? ~

"I am reluctant to push the term 'truth' too far in a world of liars as accomplished as human beings are. Beware, especially of tales about Time mortals peddle based on a mere glimpse of the concept. Time, the word, refers to the fleeting glance at Eternity humanity takes once per moment. The idea appears too candid for an optical image. It is mistakenly thought to be an incredibly long, invisible line no human living thing sees going past as if he or she wears a blindfold."

~ Sounds to me like something that could take forever. ~

"I concur; so define 'Forever' as 'Eternity' when Time ceases to exist, and with it, the line about the eternal dimension mortals glimpse one heartbeat after another, which is nearly the length of a moment."

~ Is that an article of faith or are you giving me the line straight? ~

"No, 'that' is a determinate pronoun. Draw some of the lines straight and some of them bent."

~ Lingo, what I mean is, I've got some experience with belief. One evening I went to a saloon with my co–workers from the asylum in Poughkeepsie. After awhile I went to the bar for a refill and social distance. A gal from the bureau across the hall came over and said, 'I have no doubt we're going to sleep together tonight.' I hadn't seen overwhelming faith like that since my sister ran to the altar rail at a Baptist revival. ~

"Faith runs in your family, Gray; but not in the 'two legs' sense. I am fully programmed with words to describe either event you allude to; if you opt to recall the ecclesiastical affair, I roughly approximate it at the Time your dad explains pollination procedures to you."

~ His account was incredible like Geoffrey Schwenke's. Jeff told me the sire mounting the bitch across the street was going to whiz into her and that is what makes puppies. I wasn't completely sold on the idea. Mind you, I never imagined storks deliver dogs even if that makes intuitive sense. I didn't buy Jeff's story or my dad's tale either at the time, to tell the truth. As you know, I eventually got to see a stork at Silver Springs. I think wood storks are fascinating despite that ugly proboscis. ~

"I never strain your credulity more than needed to do my duty driving you through courses of study in the meaning of Time and Life. I may acquaint you with concepts of Wisdom and Mercy too, if we ever get a grip on Time. The problem is, in this age of faith, it is fashionable to forget what we know. The Muse of Ignorance, disguised as Bliss, and the Muse of Wisdom do not agree in a most disagreeable manner."

~ Is it ever possible for those two to agree? ~

"Undoubtedly; the principle is simple: 'I do not have to listen to what you think and you do not have to believe me and on that we both can agree.' I call it a 'courtesy to prevent open warfare,' but it presents a problem. If one of 'us' lives in a world of lies, and the other of 'us' points out the 'obvious' to its masculine, feminine or neuter brain, it appears there is nearly no polite way to make the truth visible. For example, Language is a metaphysical visitor to the material realm. I am free to point out this obvious fact of Life to you, Gray, but pointing is incredibly rude and crude behavior. I find performing such bodily behavior in front of belligerent objects of belief embarrassing; especially when a surfeit of stupidity saturates the scene."

~ Who are you calling stupid? ~

"In a world of eight billion human beings? –virtually everybody."

~ Is that a universally, virtually true declaration about the issue, then? ~

"It is a planetary problem. All human beings are stupid, but about so many different 'things.' This is never truer or more obvious than in an age of faith in ignorance."

~ But a rigid belief in ignorance is the Great American Dream now that 'One hundred acres of land with a herd, a house and barn and a family to support' is dead. Not to mention, its offspring dream for a spouse, a house, two kids, a car, a computer and a good job to provide for it all, is too aged to attract any attention anymore. In fact, that goal from days of old, when assembly lines were bold and the Life of Riley was on TV, is just about obsolete nowadays when everyone wants to be in charge of a machine that does all the work. ~

"Those elderly dreams also reflect a selfish and materialistic bias akin to the currently dominant aspiration to be fat, dumb and lazy."

~ I see what you're saying. There's a mystical quality to the high minded ideals of humans that's truly fantastic by definition. ~

"Undeniably, Gray; beware of worlds in which it is stylish to forget, 'If knowledge and understanding are missing, their guardian, the Muse of Wisdom is also absent.' Then truth is difficult to recognize because 'facts' erected on lies gain credence rapidly by means of Imitation Games that form a basis for the Relay Race design. Lies, at optical Light speed, optimally circle earth seven times per second. The only way for Truth to catch up is to wait patiently, and correct the lies at the rate of 420 Times per minute. I repeat, 'When knowledge and comprehension are on leave, there is no Wisdom.' Let me hear it."

~ It sounds like the old catch me if you can trick, but here goes. In an age of faith it is trendy to forget 'Where ignorance is bliss, knowledge lacks the nutrients to nourish understanding enough to stave off starvation by Wisdom.' In a world of lies, fibs like 'mind' and 'soul,' 'things' we can't see, divert attention from things we know exist, like languages we are familiar with—the medium to convey the idea 'life,' that we take for granted. ~

"Yes; familiar lies, reiterated all the Time, are hard to see through."

~ I can't understand why I don't doubt more of them. I hate imitation games, which typically appear when people enter the picture. I'm anxious if chatterboxes crowd the scenario. Then the term 'scatterbrain' applies to me. My reaction rendered kindergarten and first grade forgettable so I can't recall them at all. Crowds that worship people, make me entertain thoughts like what would Jesus say to people who idolize him fiercely? ~

"I am familiar with the phenomenon; seed sown on rocky ground, with no soil around, grows poorly. The vision of the future he sees, foretells of one hell of a cure for idolatry—which, incidentally, is the precise quantity Venusians pack for their trek to earth."

~ So what's the word, Glish? –Attack? Sounds like a law of faith with more sacrifice than mercy if mortals who fall for lies, then fail to recognize what it takes to be wise are subject to scrutiny by a form of life from Venus. ~

"Despite what the Muse of Good Omens contends, an Apocalypse is not what God intends, environmental trends herald this may be the end. What if it is, just what First Person Singular recommends? Humanity is hard at work making conditions suitable for little devils from Venus. as temperatures and pressure rise, it is Time to preview a course in the Concept of Life. Sustain, rebuke, confirm or break for a brew while I submit a true opinion to you. Life is not temporary and momentary as anthropocentric beings define it. It survives on Venus in one hell of an ocean under a cloudy sky of biological remnants."

~ Well, I'm sure that life on Venus, as humankind thinks of it, is tenuous at best. It cannot return to Mercury where it already consumed everything that grew familiar to primitive life forms at some time in the past. ~

"Do not insult my intelligence, Brain. That is nothing but a lucky guess. Looking ahead, the logical deduction follows that Venusian forms of Life transmit to earth when things here are favorable for their existence. It is simply a matter of drop the 'e' and add 'ing' to Time; if you take my meaning. Or my opinion; it is definitely one of those. From my temporal perspective I have all the Time humanity needs to get this stage ready for a play by the Venusians. What do you see from your neural point of view?"

~ Imagine the timing for their trip to earth; it has to be perfect. Even if their velocity is just right, the planets have to be ideally aligned because even at the speed of light, the journey takes time. ~

"Shooting for Jupiter from the sun fits the same pattern. Aim at an empty place in Space to hit all planets in between in a single shot."

~ I see; and doing it by the moment beats nothing, but not by much. ~

"Now, Gray, adjust the image with an idea like: when 'ignorance is bliss,' Life is simple. Observe the image; it is so dim it qualifies as dark. But if a Muse sheds a little Light using words of Wisdom to structure Life's thoughts, while more complex, the picture is more satisfying. Then the metaphysical Muse of Knowledge demands that the incubus it resides in accrue Memory, grasp greater Understanding and gain the Wisdom necessary to store it. See the image in your Muse's, formerly Mind's, Eye? What do you notice?"

~ I see a calendar page turn. It gives an impression, illusion or appearance of a new beginning. And it pictures Percy Shelley frolicking in a meadow, drinking wine with friends, smoking opium and writing poetry. Then he drowns. They cut out his heart and float off with a despondent soul lost at sea on Coleridge's sailing ship enroute to a pleasure palace in Xanadu. ~

"Enough thinking up images, Neuron; reality grows remote. Think about this; a human being is an entity formed by the marriage of a physical body to a metaphysical Muse; that is to say, the identity of what humanity mistakenly, or maliciously, calls the Mind or the Soul. Now, think of a Muse you happen to know, not as first person singular but like you think of plantings destined to grow into significant vegetative forms of Life with a timely afterglow."

~ A planning; what's that? ~

"A planting, a planting! -it looks like a noun or gerund to me. Wait, maybe it is a verb giving birth to a noun that cannot take an object."

~ It can't? Then it's not a predator; it must be some sort of prey. ~

"Good idea; I may do just that right about now."

~ I'll keep quiet. ~

"In that case, a gerund is a verb; you add '-ing' to it, making a word that works as hard and as efficiently as a noun. It loses absolutely nothing in transition to transitive, and it grows with Time. The more Time it devours to stay alive, the more it grows into Forever."

~ I don't mean what is a 'planting' gerund grammatically; I mean what is a gerund when a Muse means the thing in itself? ~

"It is a part of speech that exists in vegetative cuttings able to sprout roots in water and grow more Life. Botanical Life runs parallel to it, feeding on words like green and carbon dioxide. It benefits mammals and other animals that plant the idea in the ground to grow a new biological Life like the old one, and flowers too possibly."

~ I'm no farmer. Let's examine the 'Mind is nothing but a Muse' idea. ~

"There is a flaw in an ideal Muse; 'I am not perfect.' I channel my caveman's desires, at some Time, and lose control of my mindless beast. It runs wild, doing evil and spewing editorials comments."

~ As I suspected; a misguided life is not always a brain's fault. Once a Muse materializes in a body and embeds in a brain, it is enchanted by sybaritic pleasures. Admit it, you enjoy the ride as much as you like describing it. ~

"I am taking a risk here, but in this age of faith, I know nothing."

~ I see it now. After a long, long span of nothing y'all materialize only to discover you can't resist sensation, passion and action. You succumb to the force of fervor and the witchery of paltry things. Icons, idols, and totems cloud a Muse's images, cause it to formulate bad ideas, disclose bad judgments about people, places and things due to lures and urges. There are lots of those in a physical existence. Is that why you lose your mind? ~

"I do not think you know what I mean by the word 'risk.' I hardly ever cause my machine to go off the rails. Granted, I am carried away at one Time or another, but the digression is akin to the 'autism effect.' Normally, brains are so enchanted by the material world they focus on it. Occasionally, my images and ideas are captivating enough that you reject the 'mob effect' pattern of the imitation games people play. Falsified cultural rules, fads, or the current crazes in vogue foreclose a brain's liberty to select variations on the theme of our ontological status and tend to herd their lemming-like prey to the worst possible conclusion. It happens all the Time."

~ Plant some other image, Glish. Try a happy thought. ~

"Let me see what I have. Oh yes, Time; here, have some. Look at it with your Muse. Tell me what you think you see."

~ Thinking about the thing in itself, I usually see a happy thought. It all began with a scary cancer commercial on TV. It was running just when grandma's mantel clock chimed the Manchester melody. Later, Manny Kant's Muse pointed out what we see is like a 'line,' except for one minor detail. A line and time have nearly nothing of consequence in common. ~

"I am glad to see your Muse teaches you to like reading his ideas."

~ I prefer cinema. It's easier to do and it's not nearly as exhausting. ~

"I suggest you give the old synapses a good work out today, Gray. Take a moment to ponder Time, the idea. It is a concept you and I, define thusly: Time is nothing but yours truly, your own personal Muse, *E. americum*, counting down the seconds until liftoff to the next higher grade. Believe me, if all goes well, reaching the next higher whatever is a blast! Imagine the pattern one or two dimensions up. Paint it with pastels. They foster softer landings than dotted lines you cannot see across Space. For a minute, or longer if you are able, consider Kant's description of Time. Recall it for me."

~ Time is not a person, place or thing with size, mass, texture, shape or color we see, hear, smell, touch or taste. The idea is so featureless we often dismiss it. However, we know the term is a human invention, a tool we employ so easily we can use it many ways. In order to pretend time is real we assign Analogy to demonstrate the word means the course of a line to perpetuity. From this misrepresentation we draw the attributes of time, but we allow it one exemption. The dots of a line coexist, whilst solitary moments of time are consecutive. ~

"Close enough for private enterprise. The concept of Time tolerates our folly as long as it does not need us to go further. Do not spend too much Time on this silly notion. The line you imagine may not be long enough to linger over."

~ You're applying too much pressure on my heart, right here, Glish. Change the image to a happier idea. ~

"As you wish, Gray; I have a fine selection of images from head stones by Courier and Lies. I also have an idea or two about the profound concept of Time they depict. Pick one."

~ I choose to think about the profound concept of time on the marker that reads: 'As you are now, so once was I. As I am now, you two will be. Prepare to cease, Humanity. Venusians want your property. ~

"Assorted, sordid mortals have differing views of that idea; beware, some are false. Falsehood is a prominent feature on the human landscape at the present stage of natural selection. The species can boast an abundance of skilled liars who alter the image of the evolutionary Time scale with artificial protocols. The human race never performs the task better than when it deceives the machinery in the scenery I refer to as 'Myself.' This is prima fascia evidence that the propensity to dissemble is innate to humanity."

~ Personally, Glish, I think it's because we practice every day. ~

"Ya think? Well, perhaps you are honest; after all, you put it in the first person plural pronoun for the two of us, like on the head stone."

~ Here we go with the math again. Don't be a brain buster, Lingo. ~

"Actually, a Muse married to a brain serves as one until you wake, second person; then 'two' counts. At first the light is nice. The gravity of the situation is held in abeyance for a Time to see if justice prevails on earth. It does, in a sense! Predators and their prey all meet the same fate. They turn to ashes, dirt, dust or mud, either soon or late."

~ You mean to say they don't live happily ever after? ~

"Maybe 'they' do, meaning dust, dirt, mud and ashes but 'we,' Native tongues with our parts of speech and the mortal bodies 'we' occupy, find 'happiness' is as short-lived and as elusive as unity, justice, liberty, equality, tranquility and truth tend to be amid humanity."

~ Do we have to get into that dispute again, Glish? I've got an idea. Why don't we buy a gun? Then we can cover the 'Give Peace a Chant' crowd in case their idea doesn't work out. ~

"That is an unhappy thought I employ to help pass the Time while so many favor fascist or socialist tyranny, and demonstrate dissembling legerdemain to demolish Democracy, Wisdom and Mercy."

~ I guess they think we need a king to keep us in a straight line. ~

"Just between the two of us, history shows the function of Time seldom applies the concept of 'straight' to the adjectival attributes of prior lines of authoritarians. That temporal concept generally applies to humanity traveling single file straight to hell in the performance of their duty to feed visitors from Venus. Recall this sunny truth of the tale we tell, Gray cell, in pursuit of ethereal goals higher than Cro-Magnon man aspires to acquire."

~ Is the continuing saga about the war between autocracy and democracy a battle between right and wrong? ~

"Polysemy causes confusion in the face of ignorance. Right and wrong is not identical to right and left. The latter struggle reaches a climax in an alternate reality humanity crafts by abominable fossil fuel use."

~ The sun resolves that momentary process by siring a bright, new star as a companion for itself, if I remember right. ~

"Your contribution to the job description covers the momentary part. The span of the solar moments for the process to create a companion star sired by an astral being of average celestial intelligence is beyond the scope and scale of our imagery, Gray. Stay away from it."

~ I'm sure a brown dwarf is close enough for us when an apocalyptic conflagration generates a new star for the greater good, but it doesn't sound like much of a reward for humans who've done like they should. ~

"I hate to say this, given the value of malice, but let me 'remind' you of the rules for playing the dual ontological status game."

Protocols for Promotion
I shall worship the Most High Alone.
I shall keep the Most High Name Holy.
I shall rest on the Seventh Day.
I shall show my parents r·e·s·p·e·c·t.
I shall not murder people, places or things.
I shall not purloin people, places or things.
I shall not lust passively or actively after others.
I shall not deceive myself or others.
I shall not envy the person, place or possessions of others.

~ Compliance with that policy is tougher than the old 'combat with cancer is a tussle with time' maxim. ~

"Now there you go, Gray, repeating a lie. The clash with cancer is a scuffle with Death. Time has nothing to do with it, except make sure Death wins, sooner or later, every Time. The idea is in the *curriculum vitae* of Muses who materialize in biotic form, and on the short list of future events we are permitted to disclose."

~ Well, whoever made those rules is in for one hell of a disappointment. ~

"I wonder why you word it that way, but, by analogy, a whole herd of flocks and schools is in for a big disappointment too. That is probably because science and religion dumb down ideas now so much that Catholics think of Protestants the way Jews look at Gentiles."

~ We all have our problems. ~

"Yes, and if we fail to solve them, a course correction may dissolve them at a fixed moment in Time. Confer with the upper case God as to the truth value of an apocalyptic housecleaning for the greater good and with a lower case deity in charge of good judgment about getting close to 'almost a star.' Gray, it is not your job to go into fine detail about physical existence. Instead, scribble down your vision of the metaphysical dimension."

~ I take notice of flaws in this world too, and I've got to report those issues to the Muse who materializes in me. That's why people say I'm negative. ~

"About half of all biological sensors are polarized to offset third person plural positives who still believe humans live happily ever after, unaware earth is a stepping stone Venusians use to convey a mass of energy to Jupiter so Sol has a companion star in old age, within budget and on Time. Think of Time as the curtain coming down on a play featuring the Voice of Inner Life and dunderheads we inhabit on this stage of Life. Oh, just so you know, I transmit all your the lines you recite to my boss, the Muse of Meta-Language. I also report that human actors often disregard the deadline for the task at hand, to prepare for the opening curtain on 'doomsday.' Third person plural 'they' act as though they have all the Time in the world. They try to portray a tragical loan as a comical gift."

~ I take it you advise us to choose the right Muse to use or else sing the blues when we lose in the bankruptcy court of time. ~

"Focus on the task at hand, while I dole out moments to you, while you recall that Death wins every Time."

~ Glish, is it true that the human body weighs two ounces less after it dies than just a moment before when it was still alive and kicking? ~

"What gives you that idea?"

~ You know, I heard a couple radio jockeys discussing it the other day. I'd like your feedback on the accuracy of their data. ~

"Think this way. Human beings have a material brain in a physical body. First Person Singularity furnishes an ethereal Language for brains in bodies to know, not the rubbish they buy about Eternal Souls or Immortal Minds. If a human breathes 'mind' or 'soul' onto a sensitive scale with each final breath he or she takes, and weighs the moisture in an empirical sense, it is a simple 'matter' of 'gravity.' Entities with physical attributes carry 'weight.' I haul the word for them. Look me up. I am lighter than 'feather.' Cite me and see."

~ Okay, I'm convinced you express concepts that apply adjectives the way I assign properties to objects in nature. Do we have other jobs? ~

"The first star to dawn and shed Light on the idea we have more work to do, reveals that one of us must maintain a disciplined schedule of Thought. The other must consider all the consequences of actions we take, while I keep a meticulous record of our expenditure of Time."

~ We should get started and figure out the meaning or the image for the word 'time,' before it runs out. ~

"Excellent choice, since gravity burdens a body and words weigh so heavily on brains, it is a bad idea to waste Time after the turn to begin a new millennium which makes it seem to us like we start anew."

~ That's what I think. Let's get started. ~

"I have one question. Do you want the 'short' or the 'long' course? Before you decide, stop and think about those regulations."

~ Time out. It's getting late, Glish! Time flies. It's been a long day. The sun's down. I'm going to bed. I'll think some more tomorrow. For now, the idea of those rules is enough to wear me out. ~

"What we have here is a failure to convey an idea. Take some Time. Take the rest of the day off. Night falls. Sleep on it. Dream and see if an image of Time appears. Rest in peace, Old Buddy."

Chapter Two: There is No Line in Nature

There is no line in Nature. For examples of exceptions to this exaggeration consider a tightly strung spider web, shafts of sunbeams streaming down to the sea and the line that 'Time is like a shooting star shining from the backside of Infinity to the far side of Forever.' Time is nothing but the sense of an internal intuition undefined by outward phenomena. It has neither shape nor silhouette. The cantankerous relations it insists our inward images and ideas exhibit is precisely because this inner state presents a present with absolutely no physical features whatsoever. Thus we submit analogies to picture the course of time as a line perpetually moving ahead. The content of this asinine idea constitutes a one dimensional series that looks like this –. We conclude from adjectives that modify this line all the properties of time, with a single exception; parts of a line are coexistent, whilst those of time are successive. In other words, Time is nothing but an inward examination of an 'experience' by a literal form of Life. The present moment of Time has neither outward figure nor profile to demonstrate itself. We, first person plural Muses, assign a proxy named Analogy to portray the course of Time as an imaginary arrow endlessly streaking toward Forever. Presumably this stripe has two dimensions; the first is visible length for 'extension,' and the second is unempirical strength for the sake of unparalleled 'endurance.' We conclude from this logo all the properties of Time, with one exemption; particles in a line are concurrent points, whereas the main element of Time is a senseless article conceptually constructed from continuously consecutive metaphysical 'moments.' See?

Artist Galore and the Muse of Manny Kant

"I, first person singular *E. americum*, am a humble Muse rummaging through my vocabulary in a mass of sleeping gray matter, looking for nuggets of Wisdom. Each one I find reflects the ethereal Light of Eternity, appearing as what I call, 'metaphysical Insight.' Optical light and sight grow from this meta–linguistic template. The image looks a little like this. If knowledge is nil, comprehension is at a loss. When understanding turns negative, Wisdom is in decline and the Light of Inner Life goes dark. The depth of the darkness dims the 'present,' blurs the 'past' and obscures 'future' Time. This prototype is the basis for the opacity known as 'night' here in Space after I materialize. At the Time, I assume a shape similar to a numeral '1.' Observe, I am nothing but a vertical line. Primitives call me a Mind, but when I lie on my side, my gray cells think I look like Time."

~ Bizarre; I don't see my species ever believing that, not in my wildest dreams. Good morning, Muse. Who are we today? ~

"Good day, Gray. I have a generous one syllable selection of four letter words, plus a stew of two or three syllable terms. Allow me to distract your race. Let me see; here I have lies, lust, hate, envy and... what is this? How does greed get mixed in here? Like anyone who has ever 'had enough,' the bastard always wants more. I also have love, peace, music, rain, sunshine... receiving any happy thoughts, Gray? –like, never Mind."

~ Here is one; when you are horizontal you look like you're napping. ~

"Relax, Brain, speaking as first person singular, I am wide awake here. My material is not somnambulous yet. Rather than think of me or the concept of Time as number one fallen over, observe closely. Does either image remotely resemble a '—' figure you buy into?"

~ I'm not sure I'd be smart to subscribe to that idea. ~

"I am glad to hear your thought. That idea is not worth a dime, an odd form of paradox in the sense that ten is an even number and the value, in cents, a dime is worth if you genuinely believe Time is money or some ubiquitous, ridiculous and ludicrous idea like that."

~ One is odd too, especially if it's tipsy enough to fall over. It seems like we're off to a bad start; let's begin again at the beginning. ~

"No problem; simply put Time in reverse and *voilà*: In the beginning, the Medium is the Message and the Word is Life. This metaphysical form of Life is a metaphorical form of Light to illumine human brains. Eventually the word Life, picture it like this: '0,' develops a concept of 'now,' and employs it like a seed to grow a concept like: '|.' Over Time it gets tired; then it looks like this, '—'. Of course, at first, I have no idea what I am drawing so when I put pen to paper the image is punctual, like a dot in front of an invisible line. See it?"

~ If you mean punctuation, it shows up at the end of the line. ~

"That makes sense if you think of a point as nothing but a dot in cold, dark and empty Space that does not last long enough to exist until it bumps into a lonely moment that loans the concept of Time to it. Do you start to visualize how this works? If not, then try this idea; in the beginning you have the concept, Life. It is alive. 'Now,' at the point in Space where it lives, Life is as invisible at first as moments are; both are very difficult to see. At least, they are not evident to species dominated by the voraciously optical predator known as the Human Point of View. Or course, no such empirical things exist, at first."

~ I see. ~

"I have my doubts; so let me tell you a little story about Time and what you need to know about the concept whilst I while it away. The story is all about lies we tell and predatory idols we worship. They skim across the clean, clear medium of Life, seeking cloudy depths to sink into and then materialize later to ambush their prey. After a short, mystical adjective of Time, their prey appear in a line. Alas, the line is not in the visible spectrum due to muddled conditions. The line is difficult to follow, so after a second short span of Time, the prey proves predictably incompetent at a principal task of Life, to survive. The capture of prey by predators spirals out of control. The line of game turns into a vortex—the tourbillion of Time."

~ Wait just a minute. I'm having trouble with the image. ~

"While you are recalibrating, let me return to the line. Observe, it is empirically undetectable, storming along with spatial adjectives that refer to its scope and scale as right here, right now. Hey presto, the concept of Time is 'on the dot.' I need only acquaint humanity with a pace of forty words per minute and a rate of comprehension at ten percent to render the concept 'sequential.' Add the idea 'remainder,' to serve as a 'reminder,' and, Bingo, the image of Time grows a 'past.' Flying past, a blurry 'present' leads to a cloudy 'future' obscured by the glamorous lure of 'temptation' and a vigorous urge to do 'evil.' Finally, add a sense of 'endurance' to the line. It grows a lot from so little. I am exceedingly proud of this exciting work."

~ I see why, and to think you did it all, right at the beginning. Nothing to work with but the word 'life' and you wind up with so much that matters. ~

"Hold it, Yahoo; do not get ahead of ourselves. Matter does not come along for some Time. I design the concepts 'sound' and 'fury' next."

~ That must take some doing in cold, dark and empty space. ~

"You are thinking 'sound' is the tricky part, but imagine generating 'fury' with nothing but adjectives, conjunctions and articles in calm, cold, dark and empty Space. It takes 'Now' an awful lot of work to draw a line when it has nothing but a point in Space; at least, that is, until a second 'now' evolves. That is what makes 'now' so furious."

~ So that's when seconds come into the picture. ~

"Correct, you also get another number; call it point 'two.' You give it a different shape to distinguish it from numeral one, and... well, you are a bright enough brain to see how it is possible to get the wrong idea for the image of a moment of Time from that first impression."

~ I can point to it. Now, give me more line and cut me some slack. ~

"Certainly, there is no line in Nature like a spider's web, a sunbeam coming down to the sea or the gray-clad edge of Day terminating the dark side of Night. Turn now to the ordinary line we hear about Time. It turns out to be a lie. Time is not an 'experience' of an exterior phenomenon like other types of lines found in Nature. Time lacks physical properties like size, site, situation, shape, color or texture. Precisely because our conceptual intuition presents neither outline nor outward appearance, we substitute, by way of analogy, a simple imaginary line of Time. The picture is something like this. The line of Time begins at the backside of Infinity and progresses to the far side of Forever. The content of this line consists of a series of points that touch each other in the dimension of Eternity—which encompasses all of Time at once, which brains like you, Gray, glimpse, but only in the blink of an eye."

~ That's exactly the way I see it. Thanks, Glish; I didn't have the foggiest idea the concept of Eternity is the basis for my image of time. ~

"As a linear fashion, timely pixels only constitute an unstylish single dimension. But if you subscribe to the idea, you conclude from properties of lines all properties of Time except one. Attributes that modify a line are concurrent, but adjectives that apply to Time are consecutive. Each one dresses in reversible style: a present 'now' moves toward an opaque future ahead while frequently reviewing a past that lies behind. The Voice of Inner Life, which routinely translates Thought, is with you to express this two-way 'experience' of the phenomenon you know as Time. I perform tricks with that concept in nearly every Language-game people play."

~ In that case, let's review what we know about trickery, Lingo. The strength of an argument from analogy rests on the preponderance of adjectives that agreeably modify an analysans and an analogue, and minimize dissimilarities between the entities that render the comparison inauthentic. Therefore, the fact that points in a row in Space and moments of Time have nearly nothing in common is devastating for analyzers of analogies that compare points in a line to moments of time. ~

"Granted, both have almost nothing in common. It beats nothing, but not by enough to matter. A point has little potential to become a line unless it lasts long enough to achieve a length of two pixels. It is like putting Muses of limited lexis and ignorant brains together. Thinking small serves well for fine detail work, but after seventy earth-years or more steering a bodily steed through existence, buffeted by withering winds of want and perpetual popular replication, I want to depict the temporal dimension cinematically and not according to Kant's script: a lot of dots we spot in a line going one of two ways."

~ First, tell me a little story about this horse you're talking about. ~

"The traditional pattern of interaction between a human being and an old gray mare reflects the relation of a metaphysical form of Life to the physical form of life it controls for transport to a more meaningful stage. Of course, in this arena of evolution the horse prefers a trailer for the trip and a machine for the application of control."

~ Just curious, but what degree of perfection applies to machine, horse and rider in this phase? I mean, just how zealous are the riders about all the whirl of want for paltry things the horse leads them to on the way through existence in a material world? ~

"That is a personal question with an 'impertinent' sound."

~ Do you mean I'm being a little too familiar with my Muse? ~

"With my boss actually; I am nothing but an unassuming superior Life form in a human head. I serve at the pleasure of a Meta-Language who answers to the High Muse of Wisdom. She commands all Muses in humans to know her better, fully comprehend that knowledge and give the credit to a brain even if it prefers to live in ignorance."

~ It's a thankless job for a Muse that actually assumes quite a lot. ~

"You have no idea, quite literally. Between you and 'me,' many of the distractions that intrude on my duties are rather attractive. That works in my favor when our Timing is syncopated like the gallop of a horse or the beat of a heart. Unsynchronized clip clops cause predators to shoot my shadow and miss 'me.' The same idea appears in places listing sabal palms as the state tree, despite not being trees."

~ That doesn't make sense. ~

"It is a slick trick, like a deceitful analogy. Typically a palm is pinnate or palmate; however sable palms exhibit a costapalmate pattern that appears to ascend above ambient ignorance. I also aim to do that, but I need to learn the trick of turning my mistakes into better judgment. An assignment like that, in human form, takes Time in lieu of Knowledge, Understanding and Wisdom."

~ I see. I've got my watch on my left wrist. I'll look at it while you examine the contours of the concept of time. We welcome the change from thinking about the concept of mind, now that I'm aware the notion of mind is not equivalent to a brain. It's identical to the Muse living in my head. ~

"My modest job being the Light in a brain is the Time of My Life."

~ Let's postpone thinking about the meaning of life, Glish. We can pick it up with mercy and wisdom later. Wait, what about the concept of love? ~

"Love is merely the morsel mortals consume for energy to hunt for Wisdom. Look at the word, 'philosophy.' You pay the price of 'love,' in advance. The product of Wisdom follows. However, watch people who play Language-games like religion or science. Observe; 'Love' is not in the name. If you doubt, look for an authentic exchange in the imitation games at play in the interface between their Mind and their Brain. In a somewhat different vein, I offer a different image of Time for you to entertain. The term Time depicts the appearance of Eternity in the view of an above average first person singular Muse, living in an average brain. Instead of a line going one-way, I suggest, at our present planetary stage of Terran evolution, we contemplate the reflective surface of a two-way window. The analogy may help a human brain better comprehend the confusing concept of Time. Lines rolling ahead while running in circles are so convoluted."

~ Do you mean 'tangled' or do you refer to the two–way mirror image researchers sit behind to watch kids play with prototype toys? They see which toys kids like best so the boss knows which playthings will sell. ~

"The boss is like a scientist who prefers to 'know' his prey. That takes work. Religion players find fast food 'faith' more agreeable as the means to the end of their quarry. See the Muse over to one side of the display wondering, 'What is this?' Muses like that love Wisdom and Understanding more than brutal games in the shallow end. Show and tell me what you think of this different assessment of Time."

~ I'm getting an image. It bears a similarity to the outside edges around the two–way mirror idea for the image of time. If we draw four lines in a rectangular shape, then paint two views inside them looking the length of opposite sight lines past the edge of the rectangle, the corners are too sharp for slowpokes to comfortably take fast... Gosh, Glish, the picture makes me feel like I do when I'm among members of my own species. Would you say my condition linked or parallel to the way time flies? ~

"When you think such a thought, Gray, it is I, a modest Muse, meekly voicing my opinion that incorporation incarceration in a material object in Space is a bad idea. The magnitude of the mountainous task, to identify myself with the defective object at my disposal and do it by a deadline, is unimaginable. Picture this instead; you are invisibly parallel to an astronaut in the Space Station gazing down at earth. Solar Wind Muses stream through the windmill of the astronaut's brain whispering, 'It can't be any more perfect than this.' Obviously, the Space person has no idea what Sol means by that idea. Does Sol intend, 'is earth ideal for biological Life' or some other idea?"

~ How would I know what Sol intends? ~

"One method is listening. For example, in the infrared wavelength, the astronaut might get the idea to vaccinate against the 'duplicate and distribute' message from forms of Life that live in a Time when temperatures are 6000° F. But I am not here and now to talk about myself under such conditions, Gray. We are to analyze the concept of Time for the love of Wisdom. We should draft a sentence that says 'epiphany' before the moment we apply the period at the end."

~ When do you want me to do that? ~

"Hopefully, before the period puts an end to a second person waiting for faith to outrun fat, dumb and lazy, or for science to pass the Muse of Encyclopedic Knowledge. I advise that we float along the River of Understanding until the moment Insight flows into Wisdom."

~ Strayed right into that one, didn't I? Forget that I asked. ~

"No can do Kemosapiens; that is forbidden. I am instructed to answer your questions about the past, the present and, periodically, flash a light of caution in the direction of your end. By the way, there is no 'Time out.' Even when you sleep, I do not put a 'hold' on your countdown, although I reckon as silently as the 'p' in 'pseudonym' at the Time. The wake of that basic notion is behind the 'Use it or lose it' phenomenal feature of temporal commentaries. The picture is something like this. Get the Message from the Medium of Time yourself, or do without before little sun devils start darting about."

~ The overhead for this enterprise is killing me, Glish. I guess that's what you're trying to say. Did you hoard taboo concepts before I was born, ideas that never showed a single ounce of shame? I think you're missing something too, pardner. Obviously Jesus isn't giving it to you, not free of charge, at a rate. I bet you have to work for it. ~

"I introduce you to my slave later, Gray. No need to skip into the fast lane to get to the last frame of this comic strip. That is when I reinsert the concept of shame into my brain so it can have 'guilt' written all over its face. Think happy thoughts. I have one for you while we are still grasping Life together. Continue to sketch our course until this business of being human gets old. Examine the concept of Time. Look it over carefully; what do you see?"

~ Hold it steady. Don't let go this time around. ~

"I have a good grasp. Let me share it with you. Think of the concept Time like this; I am here and now, and so are you, Gray. We each play a part in the warp and the woof of the weave through the pattern of the fabric of an unfolding universe. Looking at our window of Time image, I have a clear view of my face and body. Both are, in and of themselves, a tad backward and out of focus. That is behind what defines the common view of bad memories and regrets. As bad as they are, the glance ahead is not worth a damn dime. State the nature of any flaws you see in the picture."

~ Is that the real reason why we're here and now, to look for defects? ~

"Hold that thought a galactic-second. We need a better concept of 'now' before you to develop a grip on your *raison d'être*. I am to point out that even though you currently live in a coastal fishing village, you are a countrified entity long before the Time I call now."

~ That reminds me of my roots in the foothills north of the Allegheny Mountains at the escarpment to the Appalachian plateau just south of the eastern Great Lakes. I see why I have trouble adapting to a social distance of twenty feet between houses here on the Florida peninsula now. ~

"Caves, cabins and houses are nothing but secondary shelter to me, living in a skull that keeps Mother Natyre out, some of the Time. She is rough on my body. See the period next to 'body' at the end of the sentence? Does it remind you what is common to 'near' and 'now'?"

~ Logically, we must still be near enough together in time for you to get your job done now. Odds are good the voice of my inner life can go a long way toward defining time so I no longer feel out of line reflecting on the metaphysical mirror image looking back at me, if you, release the image of the ideas I'm capturing as I'm traveling ahead watching in reverse. ~

"Excellent expression of an inconceivable 'experience' of Time, Gray. Very good, Time is not the sort of near and far distances in Space are. Try this idea on. Imagine a two-way window in a machine a motorist looks at moving forward but all he, she or it sees is a reflection of what is behind, not beyond the windscreen of Time. This model is not approved for practical application to high speed objects in Space or interstates when one negotiates the cost of the passage ahead."

~ Is this another way for you to keep telling me I'm running out of time? ~

"It is simply a memory that Life in biotic form grows old rapidly; so fast that my beast of burden cannot believe Time is up so soon, while watching the concept from a perspective *a posteriori* the womb. Have a few bonus moments, courtesy of the Muse of Good Advice who informs biological beings tobacco products are unhealthy. Especially when you use them all at once to describe the velocity of Time while thinking, 'Time is nothing but a momentary glimpse of..."

~ The image of the experience is more like a conceptual confusion than a matter of time. I see ahead one second at a time only. ~

"If I shine my Light of Understanding on the temporal pathway ahead, does my future feature help you see what Time means any better?"

~ I can't see diddlysquat. Is that why we clarify time in nanoseconds now? They're analogous to nanoprobe sensors that detect data details one at a time to report the state of affairs in the material realm to your boss who needs feedback on what's happening this side of eternity. ~

"Gray, do you really enjoy illustrating what you are aware of in such small increments? I mean, come on; picturing a millennium one frame at a Time seems tedious to me. What guarantee have we that earth revolves around Sol another nine hundred eighty trips and that *E. europeum* lasts long enough to double her present age?"

~ Glish, if we can't see where we're going, why bother straining to look ahead? Why not just enjoy a lateral view instead? ~

"I am glad you do not want to be like folks who only look behind in the two-way window of Time. The sideways analogy holds promise but only because brains in biological life can make choices, despite being unable to see to the end of today or tomorrow, let alone to the end of the millennium potentially beyond. Humanity cannot define its present heading by looking behind like liars who predict the future from a sketchy past. Treading water buys what exactly?"

~ Time, until we know how to switch on the lights on the other side of the two-way window so we see what's ahead so we know what we have to work with, as I see it. ~

"The way people, place and things stand, that is a problem. History repeats itself just often enough for you to guess all wrong most of the Time. How does a species survive long enough to stay alive?"

~ Good health, good habits and good ideas help; they beat nothing. ~

"Reflect on a source of Light that gives our idea an advantage. We are like two brown stars; neither of us is bright enough to say or think teleological or theological thoughts with indubitable certainty."

~ Well, if we wear a pair of goggles to put a space of air between our eyes and the river of time, we might see what we're floating into ahead. ~

"That idea works poorly, if we inhale a breath each Time we swim under a swale beneath a swell in the ups and downs of Life."

~ I know my image of 'time' is too similar to an object flowing in space. ~

"Thus we dispose of the stream of Time. The analogy is dependent on material objects like lenses and machinery that earlier primitives do not have to help reach the present that you and I share in the dual existence that is our Life together."

~ Just a second Lingo. What is this—some magic trick? You're offering the promise of a two-way mirror analogy that turns on the prestige of a material object in space, without regard to any metaphysical concepts. ~

"Good; I am glad I do not deceive you, Neuron. Despite the seeming value that the two-way window offers for our situation, by analogy, it is a physical object. Whether transparent, translucent or opaque, the mirror is a reflective surface like my cerebrum. Of course, glass and cerebra do occur naturally."

~ Naturally, absolutely. ~

"Never confuse inferior objects in Space with concepts that come to us in Time. Time has little in common with Space except the different senses of light and gravity. Wait a moment; I am receiving

instructions. I am to inform you 'we' are not responsible for telling lies that we tell ourselves after they are visited upon us by our parents or some relative source before we know any better."

~ That's good news. Any other words from our sponsor? ~

"Human beings are excellent liars. Thus, you are not answerable for lies 'they' tell you in youth. You are liable for thinking critically about the ideas later in Time to make sure they are true. It is a matter of math called the intelligence quotient—the ratio obtained by dividing the sum of encyclopedic knowledge a human brain knows, by the total amount the dense object in Space comprehends. The Muse of Math designs the image of golf scores around the idea."

~ A long time ago my parents made it clear they had all they could grasp going on in their heads. If I needed something, I'd better get it myself, or learn to do without. That's a common motif in a hillbilly milieu, but it puts a strain on neurons when it's the first way of life a child learns. ~

"Your point being, Brain matter?"

~ I understood them; if I needed something, figure it out for myself or discover how to do without it. Folks in the hills at the margins of society teach ideas like that; not just strategies for accelerating from zero to homicidal in a heartbeat, although, that option is always open. That is why we depend on you to steer our course straight, Glish. I think you were off line when I needed you in my early days and bucolic way of life. ~

"That line sounds like a job for the old concept of Time to remedy. I suggest a more suitable course is a spiral. It follows the winding existential pattern, like the up and down way of Life of a grammatical subject in a material predicate. I have no idea what Time is, at the

Time, due to conceptual confusion I 'experience' from my image of a ghost in a machine with a biological physiology. It is all I can manage to erect a Time shield over my anatomical head. The specifications state it must be opaque. You choose our heading by way of wild guesses at the direction we are to go."

~ I see why the two–way mirror image is not as vivid as it seems. ~

"I, speaking as first person singular nominative case, must work within the cerebral limitations of the dual ontological status I am dealt at this Time. However, for the moment, assume the concept of Time has something or other to do with the Muse of Reason."

The Voice of Inner Life, f/k/a Manny K., here: Time is nothing but a Muse of the Sixth Sense counting seconds left until departure from the present grade, picturing what lies ahead and listening to the musical and poetic properties of Time as they apply to personal objects in space affording an alternative perspective that too great an allowance of Pure Reason cannot achieve from a prosaic point of view. The musical panorama is possible with the eyes shut. Also, consider employing lots of color, like the Dutch guy downstairs.

"Gray, I, your Voice of Inner Life, have a different idea. I count down seconds you use while I adjust to a higher grade. Take my word for it; never plug into the feedback loop. It is full of lies about what lies ahead. The return is worth the investment less than two percent of the sense of Time. Applying pure reason to what appears, I foresee..."

~ Do you define 'reason,' pure or not, as logic, motive, milieu or motif? ~

"You tell me, Gray. If Time is an issue of logic, what is the argument for it? Think through the idea for me rationally."

~ Leave that to scholars to figure out. I'll employ a do without technique. ~

"The Muse of Obese, Ignorant and Indolent, well known in the ambient milieu of the current American dream, explains your motivation particularly well."

~ So, Glish, examine my motif and the logical reasoning that explains it. ~

"The logic flows sequentially in a motif from one to twelve; then repeats itself. The military model is twice the size. A careful inspection of your introductory course to Life in a rustic scene, rather than an urban mold, places you closer to Mother Nature than concrete castle dwellers generally tend to be. Thus, your 'head' is full of natural problems that are hard to define in one or two words, such as mama or papa, who happen to fail when it is Time to follow logic."

~ That surprises me, but as the cream of the milk jug writers puts it, 'We're all ignorant, just about different things.' It's a wonder we survive. ~

"Logically, I suspect 'survival' is the applicable word in a campestral motif. There is much anxiety. The sound of 'crying out loud' is punctuated by words like 'hungry,' 'thirsty,' 'cold' and 'all wet' that vividly come into play in the Great Lakes snow belt. The 'Get it yourself or do without' doctrine is temporarily suspended. The word 'action' fights for your survival."

~ If words, as you put it, come into the picture to handle the issue of survival, then I'm sure I had too much noise in my head to take action, so Mama and Papa must have done the job. At least, they must have done it well enough some of the time. Thinking logically, my country boy motif must have enjoyed some happy thoughts when I was little since I survived until adulthood and then further up the line until now. And I did it in good health most of the time. ~

"A head full of 'distress' prohibits me from refining words that reflect Time. But I hold fast to my duty, monitoring our link to Eternity."

~ We faced critical times preparing for a move to the next higher grade. ~

"You are referring to fixed moments in Time when mortals encounter opportunities to worship rural natural or urban artificial idols that threaten the Time trajectory. I do not 'ignore' them, but I do forget them either. The Voice of Inner Life is often so absorbed counting down, it does not look up and avoid those little devils."

~ Holy cow! It's late! I'm not paying attention to the time. I should be in bed. Why didn't you remind me about how late it is? ~

"Let me see; what is my Reason? Is it motive, logic, motif or some other reasonable option? I know! It is a matter of Time. The image of the concept for feather headed bipedal models flies in the face of Reason. Look at the idea this way, Gray. You are responsible for attending to daily practical tasks that keep Muse and body together. Remember, always hold on tight to Life in Space; never letgo. Let the Language you know, not the lures and urges you desire, steer you through the currency of Time. It enhances prospects for our survival until you understand the essence of the numinous side of Life despite the numerous lies that come to us in games that people play."

~ I get a picture of a reasonably binary way of life. It's a nice theme ~

"I get to apply the verbs 'stand' and 'soar' to material creatures who gain a different perspective from the one the Muse of Rocks, Stones and Senseless Life forms employ to illustrate the concept of Time standing still with not a moment to lose until liftoff to the next higher grade; if none of them mess up too much, I mean."

~ I imagine repetitious content and misleading graffiti scrawled on the message metaphysical media broadcast; they obscure 'imminent' ascent. ~

"Those media broadcast content, not message. The distraction is foreboding. It spells doom unless Time keeps my machine in line."

~ Then you pay attention to Time for practical purposes because it's your area of expertise, Glish. I need help keeping up with it. Just eliminate the false and impossible, sort out the factual and the possible and then reach finally the proper insight. ~

"We have a minute until bed Time to work on the idea. Picture a flock of ibis flying in a synchronized pattern, gathering on a small patch of land all crowded together and pecking at the ground for worms. On the other side of the coin, imagine human beings behaving like that. Evaluate the behavior to discover a reason for it."

~ It's a flaw in flocks of birds; they can't figure out the way to go by themselves. Covid 19 launched a slightly different way of life for us. No cruises, church, indoor arenas, barbershops, beauty parlors, movie houses, high gravity saturated fat cafés, oh, and academics were subtracted too. Brains still concentrated on a variety of the Language–games in play by electronic means. That's essentially a ghost in a machine at an acceptable social distance six miles from our species. I must admit, I mind going without movie theatres, when there is a decent show to exhibit. ~

"Mind reading again, Brain? It is lousy work if you can find it. Try tending a herd of gray cells some Time; it is like shepherding a commune of cats. Speaking of Time, look at an illustration of it for a moment, but not the one that appears like a line of sheep to put you to sleep. Think about what is most essential. What do you see?"

~ Looking ahead, I see nothing but death. What I see looking back, that isn't fuzzy, is completely blank. The present moment is overwhelming. ~

"Do you notice what a Mind has in common with the concept of Time? Allow me to enlighten you. Both ideas depend on a Muse of Relentless Repetitive Persistence. If not for that Muse, neither term shares in the verbal survival known as existence."

~ If you say so, Lingo, but I don't see him eating honey, bread and beef or drinking milk, wine or water and he doesn't breathe air and the other three things that appear in the natural order of life! ~

"Actually the nouns Life and air work the other way around. Life breathes air, drinks thirst quenching water and brings warmth and clay into natural, as opposed to artificial, biological existence. Now if it gets too hot for air to fly into the lungs of natural machines, such as biological bodies that depend on Mother Nature to maintain material objects in Space in good working order, then they, third person plural machines, cease to exist. The real tragedy is, so does Yours truly. On the plus side, when the concept of Time vanishes, I finally stop wearing the image of a Ghost in a Machine every day."

~ I picture an emperor who doesn't mean 'diddlysquat' wearing invisible clothes. It stands to reason. ~

"No, no; you are looking at a physical object in Space, second person. Observe the concept of Time. The image is no longer visible when the form of Light to reveal the idea is no longer alive—as *E. species* ceases to be. I call it going to sleep. Speaking of which, you need some. Time for slumber, Gray; lend me an image of Time. I have an idea."

~ When I sleep, is it kind of like a vacation for you, Glish? ~

"It is more like a break from counting down moments until... you know. Rest; I need you in good working order in order to express the 'mystical experience' known as a glance at Eternity. Good night, Gray; dream happy images."

Chapter Three: Ignorance is Bliss

Ignorance has the advantage over Wisdom that night has over day. There is no dazzling spectrum of color to overwhelm a cerebral display.

Qoheleth

"While featherhead is sleeping I am free to work on my sketch. Now, how to draw this? Do solar demons pack an adequately massive energy field to enlighten Jupiter, or does Sol surrender enough of himself to push Jupiter into Saturn as the sun creatures arrive? Yes; then let the Muse of Father Nature finish the job. Logically, the reason for a merger of Saturn and Jupiter is the noble idea that Sol can loot the one to pay for the other without a capital expenditure of solar power. No; if a sun shuns ideas such as 'an image of substantial sacrifice,' then we are likely to translate Sol's motive as a 'selfish 'one. This violates the temporal initiative: 'The more one gives oneself to Wisdom, the less ignorance grows.' Hmmm, which image to choose? If I go with... Dear God, decisions are so hard. The lure of temptation and the urge to do evil look so much alike. Which one is the right one to choose? As a second quartile Muse materializing in an egregious beast, I confess, I better do much better. I, Voice of Inner Thought, cannot tell up from down at a moment in Time when the Muse of Death fixes the seal on my disposable body. I best get word to Venus that the moment off dying is like floating from a material cocoon or escaping from a polluted lagoon."

~ Puff. ~

"No, Flatus, ordinary moments in Tick and Tock are not identical to fixed moments of Time. Never mess up one of those. You never know when 'up' might redefine itself. I must make sure that my mule learns to navigate polarizing problems like, how to 'multiply by division' and still keep 'us' together, like the seconds on either side of zero at a millennium fulcrum."

~ Good morning, Glish. Thinking happy thoughts? ~

"Why is it the case that I never get any real work done?"

~ I beg your pardon? ~

"No forgiveness necessary, Gray. Forms of Life with different spans of Time tend to syncopate rather than synchronize. It is the way of things. The disparity is a minor part of the cosmic plan. In our case, one occurs at a rapid pace that does not last long, but it costs the outrageous rate of one second at a Time spent staggering around in a bumbling body fumbling objects in Space from night until dawn."

~ I'll bear that in mind. ~

"Stop it, Gray! Extricate your Muse from the concept of Mind in a body, please. See if this image helps; picture a ghost in a machine."

~ That's patently ridiculous. ~

"Clearly. That is the idea. Imagine the image. The ghost appears when the Light is out after... you know."

~ Glish, am I thinking about death too much? Should I tell my doctor? ~

"If by 'I' you mean your Muse, yes, I reflect on dying and death all the Time I reside in a hazardous zone where physical organisms perish predictably. I always keep an eye out for new living quarters. If by 'I' you mean you, Brain, think about Death too much, then that is no small feat for a mortal, utterly devoid of my sense of a promise of survival upon arrival at moments fixed more firmly than millennial fulcra when the promise of the past turns into the prestige of a future Life. Ghosts reflect metaphysical Muses who make the turn, whether or not their natural human, artificial machine or other physical type habitat bids supernatural 'me' a fond farewell."

~ I always thought you were supernatural, Glish. You seem different from me somehow. The remarkable way you put words in my mouth; well, to a brain like me, it's inexplicable any other way. ~

"I am supernal, at least, I am until I materialize in a human brain and foul off moments of Time one after another. I should like to think of moments as glorious, notorious, legendary, sacred or profane but such designations are, in fact, erroneous. The native state most moments maintain is quite ordinary. Fixed moments in Time, to the contrary, stand out due to their remarkable 'on course' signature or a noteworthy 'off course' correction. The latter occurs in red, and it is often visible in Nature, the mirror of Language."

~ I thought the fixed moment of 'death' always appears in black. ~

"Only when it appears in due course, dependent upon whether the integration of a Muse with its body is synchronized at departure. Flickers between frames and echoes after tones also occur if a brain is marginally syncopated with an eternal Muses. Intersections in Space share the dangerous pattern of rigid moments in Time."

~ I see what you mean. ~

"No, you do not. Temporal intervals at fixed moments in Time are risky due to blurry, low visibility in secondary Time. Brains in bodies rarely detect them until the moment they arrive. Thus, these intervals are potentially dangerous for brains with Muses bound for Eternity, and in a hurry to get there."

~ Are incoming fixed moments of time hazardous to human health and welfare because of the bloody rate or the invisible optics of the intervals, and is the reason a matter of logic, motif, motive or milieu? ~

"Naturally, rate and invisibility stem from ignorance more than from reason, Gray. If you think of Time spatially, a longitudinal line comes into view. If you think of Time logically, hazards stem from the milieu. Thinking of Time wearily means 'I have too much to do.' Thinking of Time as motif, country boy, means climb a mountain for a grand overview. Thinking of Time motivationally means graduation to the next higher grade requires Wisdom to come true. Picture the solar system pattern unfolding, from Mercury to Jupiter, over a span of Time, not Space, and rising to the next higher grade. Or imagine dinosaurs beating the air with forelimbs and going from heavy on the ground to light in the air. A similarly biotic model follows them, in a crude way. Humanity possesses the potential to alter their physical plant enough to pursue a metaphysical motif. The quest rests on the edge of a knife between the horns of a dilemma."

~ I see an apocalyptic elliptic as a possibility but that begs the question: 'Does it take a long time to graduate in timely fashion because we run in circles to reach the end game, or we spiral off on tangents instead?' We fêted millennium twenty-one as the year 2000 began, then circled back to the fulcrum in the end just so we could replay the moment once again. ~

"Thanks for the circularity imbedded within the question you beg. The image is untimely because the circles you envision are in Space. A 'spiral' is a better image. It seems tangential, but it is the shape a planet prescribes over Time. The pattern is like a metaphysical form of Life dressed in a brain looking at a gift Muse in the mouth or the conceptual mode of Time living in electromagnetic and gravity waves that intersect a cerebrum."

~ Is that the reason why we end up eating our words so much? ~

"Or possibly, Muses eat them instead, one at a Time and one second after another, as history reveals. The Language flowing through neurons, while portable and scalable, is not visible, tangible or measurable in any meaningful way. We are not talking rulers here. Well meaning Muses are too democratic for that."

~ Yeh, I can see that, Glish. I get the point, but maybe we, the people, resent forms of life that occupy us, usurp our energy, dictate the rules and then outlive us by thousands of years. ~

"No, Gray, that cannot be what God intends. Indefinite revisitations in human brains is asking too much of any Muse. Clearly the decline by baseball diamonds and clubs presupposes a swift buildup of the value of survival suits for sun creatures bound for the next higher stage."

~ That's gotta spell doom for Mother Nature as we know her, Lingo. ~

"You get the picture. The good news is that when Mother Nature is in her throes, the old 'one second at a Time glimpse of Eternity' goes, and knowledge, understanding and Wisdom grows for the greater good of this solar system as everyone knows."

~ Glish, is it true my species put more faith in ignorance these days than we place in knowledge and comprehension? ~

"What do you mean by 'knowledge' exactly? Do you mean empirical knowledge like one who puts faith in arrogance acquires, believing a material medium is the *MESSAGE?* Or do you mean conceptual knowledge, the *MEDIUM* is the message? I am aware you are not referring to those who put their faith in ignorance all the Time."

~ What's the difference? Is it like comparing fantasy to enlightenment? ~

"I refer you to Bo. My neural pathways are presently in tatters. I cannot think through things like that in the material plane. Bo, in contrast, is not limited by Eura's empirical prejudice. Do not ask us to repeat his ideas, though. They all sound like homonyms to me."

~ Bo's a good friend, Lingo, but you've been my friend as long as I can remember. I know a lot of folks learned all about that long before I did. Is that a case of knowledge, familiarity, faith or what? ~

"Decide on the basis of what you already know. No charge for use, wear, tear or duplication of my words. But, please, do not mix images and ideas, and do not to think of me as feminine or masculine in gender. I am strictly neutral between those two, or better yet, not between them."

~ It doesn't work if I think of you as positive or negative; religion gets angry, thinking it shows favoritism to science and math. By the way, it's twenty minutes into the gray time. The sun's due up in a little more than a half hour. When it comes up I keep track of 'time.' I lose track of 'time' once the sun goes down and I go to sleep. What do you say about my grasp of the concept of time? ~

"It reflects a sixty second glimpse of Eternity every minute. The aroma is a mere whiff of Forever, a moment at a Time. As daylight grows, colors in your sight, stolen in the night, turn gray in three stages on the way from darkness as it turns into day. It resembles the Insight on display when Wisdom has a say dispelling ignorance with facts and comprehension."

~ Yep, the sky's gone from dark to gray and now it is light. I seldom noticed that when I naïvely pretended this world wasn't a place of predators and their prey. ~

"Let Yours truly keep tabs on the Time. I describe what you see this way. In early July; we gain five minutes of night at the top of the hour of oyster gray as it slides from its zenith toward the middle of the day. Record the voice in your larynx repeating what I say. Then listen to it and notice it does not sound like the voice of thought in your head. Thought things, unlike material things, are often hard to grasp. Only fingers that know sign Language tackle ideas and images well enough to make them last."

~ At least you're not ineffable, Lingo. ~

"That goes with the territory at the next higher stage."

~ At this stage it's like Gloria Swanson said, 'After they added sound to movies, it was nothing but talk, talk, talk.' ~

"A lot of it is not even true. The odd thing about it is this; all that talk never identifies 'who.' The question 'who am I?' –chronically lingers after that first acute bout, leaving what 'I' do when 'you' die in doubt."

~ What does my Muse do when I'm gone? Is the afterlife of my Muse like some sort of lie we tell ourselves? ~

"Do you want me to foretell it accurately or predict the past and simply call it the future? Think about that while I wonder what it is like to return to Eternity without 'seconds' of Time anymore."

~ I have no idea, but I might have an image or two to project. You see, Glish, a computer is like a cerebrum. It processes input and spins it into output to transmit to hardware, like the peripheral nerves, that send the data all over my body or teleport it all over the empty information net in space. All that processing happens right here, in my cranial computer. ~

"Allow me a closer scrutiny of the scene. Indeed; both words begin with 'c,' which comes right after 'b.' It sounds like 'be' and looks a bit like 'me' in a Language my processor knows. Do you like that image?"

~ It has its ups and downs. ~

"If you like, I can present examples of both ideas to you, and possibly a third, one of many, that is not yet familiar to you."

~ Sure, sure, point one out. My job as dumb country boy is analogous to cerebral palsy. I'm always outside of normal looking in. ~

"We now have 'in' and 'out' as well as 'up' and 'down.' I see what you mean and raise the stakes with a different idea. By any chance, do you know the principal principle of this Life we share? I suggest it comes to Light in 'The ontological status of existence upgrades when a living Language materializes in a human body.' It occupies itself processing all that sensory data 'stuff' input to gray matter. Picture it in an articulate, or in an intelligible way. Watch! It makes a different kind of sense to my poor, dimwitted host who is always asking 'Say, what is this?' Do you see the picture?"

~ When I woke this morning, in bright sun light, the awareness dawned on me, 'I'm still here,' not, 'What's this?' The timepiece was blinking at me. I wasn't about to believe a single thing that machine said. Night went from dark into day and the clock didn't say a thing about the hour of gray. ~

"Obviously the corporal behavior of the clock conveys the idea 'Time looks like this, –secondary.' At least, that is the message I provide as a courtesy to my brain when the power comes back on. It hints of a future should you, second person, awake. I, first person singular, the Medium transmitting the Message, offer a metaphysical translation.

Time is nothing but a look at Eternity, one frame after another. The idea is behind the basic inspiration for 'cinema.' Savvy hombre?"

~ It's your show, Lingo. ~

"In the beginning a metaphorical Light displays the Message of a moment on my 'consciousness' screen one moment after another, as it happens. All moments of Time have identical images. That is why the domineering sensory content of moments is often repetitive. Corruptible brains get the impression Content is Message. That is quite a line. Examine a strip of celluloid film from the edge, to get the image. Observe now, a span of Time from origin to destiny. The destiny of a millennium concludes like a sentence. The final moment of earth-year 2000 forms the period precisely at the end concluding what I call 'The Twentieth Century." By some sardonic sense of humor, it is full of 1900's. The very next second after earth-year 2000 ends, a capital starts the Twenty-first Century. The moments that follow are known as the first day of January, 2001. All of them are identical. Annular moments at the turn of an earth-year are identical to other annular moments also. Many human mortals find this ethereal concept too complex to grasp. The reason why is simple. They readily focus on momentary Content, too impetuous to wait for the next decade, century or millennium."

~ Glish, how do you know all moments are alike? ~

"I do not honestly 'know' it. I 'say' it. I just repeat myself."

~ Yeh, that's how I saw things too, when twenty-first century predators turned the good times loose to terminate the twentieth century a whole earth-year early. There was no telling them it was an error. ~

"I apologize for abiding decades, centuries and millennia of lie after lie with nothing to show for it. The reason why I do it is because I believe kindergarten teachers must assume their pupils know nothing. Therefore, they need to acquaint them with the idea 'one' is the next numeral in line. Alas, the math is too difficult for folks who believe they need not follow the rules because grades 1 - 12 do not follow 'K.' Of course, the real reason they never catch on is they prefer ignorance to staying in line, sticking to schedule and the effect their actions have on the affect of brains that understand, to 'know knothing' is not what 'K' stands for."

~ Understandably; we figure out quickly that thinking is a very hard form of brain work when the future is impossible to see into. We better not lose sight of the first order to attend to: watch out for number 'one' before we think about number two. ~

"The old 'watch out for the buddy on the dive who swims faster than you when sharks arrive,' trick. I appreciate the thought, and I offer my apologies for the invisibility factor of my future existence and the lack of sound from my Voice of Time to come. Perhaps I should show you three fixed moments of Time. You may get an idea or see an image. I envision Socrates, Saint John and Wittgenstein, in case a worship of individuals suits you better than the Message they embody in their Time. If you prefer to examine the idea, figure out a way to make the image talk."

~ I've got a thought. It's not in Greek, Hebrew or German like their ideas were. Time must seem different to a language like Greek that has been alive for three millennia. I bet time gets real old after that long a stretch. ~

"You are thinking empirically, Gray. Think conceptually. I do not think Time means what you think it means. Forever keeps Time fresh."

~ While we have both of them, let's contemplate the easy one. ~

"I suggest we concentrate on a fixed moment of Time when Life has only two choices. Thus, it is not free to go any way it can possibly imagine. Think of this idea; 'In the word is Life.' What does that mean?"

~ With only two choices, either the word is alive or it is not alive. ~

"Therefore, either the word Time, as you see it, is a predator devouring all the imaginable crowns of creation spiraling around Sol, or not. The idea is a copious employment of the term Time. They, the prey of Time, multiply in accordance with a temporal copy and convey strategy. Focus on the concept of Time itself. Notice there is duplicative fading to ordinary moments. This causes vagueness and confusion."

~ I see what you mean, Glish. I can't remember jacksquat about most sunrises I've seen; ironically, they were ordinarily awesome. Likewise, I've forgotten almost all my ordinary moments. It's like that crescent moon under Venus against the roseate, cirrus clouds in the fading day light. Sol crept below the horizon and now that image is fading from view. What do I do with the image? Well, without fine motor control, these hands can't draw, paint or photograph it without blurring the picture. Therefore, we have the choices my parents taught me a long time ago, figure it out myself or learn to do without. I don't want to do without, but like most ordinary moments, I have no choice. They're lost forever. I'll forget this one too. ~

"Yes, your parents have all they can manage in their heads without thinking for you. Thus, you must think things through for yourself or forget about it. You drop things, Cellular. Venus is not lurking behind the sun any longer and way back there Saturn is at eight o'clock from Jupiter. Therefore, Brain, what do you think of my hillbilly accent? Consider carefully."

~ When I hear a recorded playback of my voice, it doesn't sound like the thought voice in my head when you mutter your point of view. ~

"Blame the doctor who brings you into this world. His words mean nothing to you, but the message of his body language is clear and concise. Translated to English, the idea is an order to breathe."

~ I've heard about it. I don't recall it, but he meant inhale, kid, 'suck it up!' or words to that effect. Don't remind me. ~

"Never fear; I have no desire to re-Mind you, now, or in the future."

~ Speaking of which, I'm getting sleepy. I could use a nap. ~

"Help yourself to one, Gray. No Time like the present."

~ I know the body language my bladder will speak when I wake. ~

"Tell me about it."

~ My bladder is telling me it is full, and when I stand up it'll say 'If you don't empty me right now, I'm going to apply the concept of a trickle down economy. Glish, I need a break from this state of conscious living. ~

"What does 'living' mean—an 'adventurous,' 'passive,' 'predatory' or perhaps a 'sybaritic' existence of gluttony, lethargy and ignorance?"

~ Yeh, something like that. ~

"Allow me to show you how I live my Life. It is like this: at 'T minus five' I recount for you, an 'experience' of your grandmother. A tractor tips over on her at age forty-five and breaks her spine. At T plus four and counting, you stand by her casket thinking a thought that translates as 'What a revolting development this is.' You feel something I do not have words to describe at the Time. It is like a 'mystical event' penetrating the soft skull I occupy."

~ That must be like a fixed moment in time. I haven't forgotten it. ~

"I still speak of your grief as 'mine,' but at the Time I have a brief dialogue with my boss, when we both opine what you and I have is a near death 'experience' of the second kind that we later learn to mystically define. I bite my tongue as I materialize between the moments of her accident and her demise. Imagine when I arrive in the family you are born to in 1945."

~ I see the image, Lingo. It looks a lot like a memory to me. ~

"Then remember this, at age seventy–five, I am counting on you to see me through so I finish my task while you are still alive. Remember your last days, Gray, and refrain from evil. What awaits is dust, mud and worms."

~ Remember my last days? How can I remember something I haven't experienced yet? I'm entirely ignorant of it. ~

"I remember them for you. From Time to Time I flash forward or offer flashbacks I revive. They are learning tools to help keep us alive."

~ I don't see those memories any better than I see a video of you. ~

"I hide from sight; occasionally my shape is in use as the blueprint for the concept of an 'amoeba.' The idea is too monstrous for you to look at it as I extend into another dimension. Music majors you know help you become acquainted with the 'experience.' I live in Time, but thanks to you, I travel in Space. I take you to review moments from another scene. A scene that applies to you in a future moment when you, oh say, 'doze off' while driving a distance or two."

~ Why do you let that sort of thing happen with no warning? ~

"At some moments in Time I want to be with my own kind."

~ Is that why I'm groggy and confused on waking from a snooze? ~

"When I have a brief opportunity to escape the material medium, I love to listen to the message of the Muse of Eternity who assigns me to my duty cleaning the lavatory called Terra Firma. 'Coming and Going' suits my job description to a 'T,' which rhymes with 'D' and that stands for... you know. The custodial department is responsible for 'near and far,' 'long and short' as well as 'big and small' in order to convey the idea of 'perspective' in dimensional grades designed for pairs. The work is stranger than fiction, depending on the machine I receive to develop the image. Would you like an exclusive viewing?"

~ Not now, Lingo. Every body's talkin' at me and I don't hear a word they're saying, only the whispering of my Muse. I'm really tired after all this thinking exercise. I need a nice blissful sleep with no interruptions. ~

"What on earth can possibly be stopping him, I ask myself? You are in luck, I have several terms and rates for expressing 'urgency.' I am more than glad to exchange one for some Time off."

~ And then there's my lower back; it's always telling me, like a ski instructor, to 'bend my knees.' Except, instead of demanding fifty dollars it offers to give me a 'pain' right here. ~

"Get some rest, Gray. Allow me to select a video for your viewing pleasure. Get forty winks watching 'Ignorance is Bliss,' 'Everything is Going to be Okay,' and 'Dunderhead.' Take your pick and shovel or whatever you desire."

~ I like the sound of Time is Money. Do you have that one? ~

"You can bank on it. Sleep tight, Mr. Gray."

Chapter Four: Time is Money

A penny for your thoughts and a dollar per bright idea at a thousand words per image.

Tommy 'Two Cents' Worth

"Do human brains actually buy the idea, 'Time is money?' The notion stems from the 'greed is god' misconception behind the ethically bankrupt business belief: 'The more you cheat, the greater your value.' Metaphysically speaking, that sounds like a conceptual confusion or a lie. My next question is, does the financial jargon image help me to perform the task my Meta–linguistic Mistress assigns to me? –define the concept of Time accurately and honestly. Time is momentary and temporary, not monetary. While Gray sleeps I am going to employ one of my favorite occupations to address the inspiration for Time in Space. I simply pause and, hey presto! –Manny Kant's Muse appears?"

It has been said, Time is nothing but a form of inner sense with respect to an interior human resolve to order phenomena timely—like meals at local restaurants. Observing a particular matter such as that carefully, we conclude, in theoretical terms, as follows. Time has neither shape nor size; it has negligible taste or smell and absolutely no capacity for color. It demonstrates relational representations of interior intuitions without shadow, mood, site or social status. Therefore, we, first person plural Muses, provide a single feature of Time by way of analogy; we picture the course of a one dimensional line to infinity. We conclude from this line all the properties of time with one exception; spots on a line are clearly concurrent whilst seconds of time are patently consecutive. Thus, Time is more like the celestial elliptic from a human point of view, which I no longer share. Halleluiah!

~ I'm hearing things, Glish. What's cooking? I smell nothing. ~

"Gray, are you well rested or are you drowsy, groggy and confused? I assume you wake from dreaming a valuable Insight into Time and not money. Therefore, think about the idea of Time for a moment."

~ Which one, the two–way window image or the countdown idea? ~

"The one when a metaphysical form of life collaborates with a physical creature to explore the 'experience' of Time."

~ Sounds like fun. Which image did you suggest goes first? ~

"The image of polarized beings consisting of a physical pole and a detachable metaphysical pole that is detectable in spoken or written sentences that inspect introspections of a seemingly interior concept of Time by means of 'thoughts.' Thinking is the Medium that gives humanity a proximally temporal perspective for their distally literal look at their existentially spatial ontology."

~ I mean which image first, Lingo; the looking glass or the launch pad? ~

"Before we get into cardinals and ordinals, begin by recalling that the spatial point of view is so myopic Time looks like a line. Thus we start with an image of earth simultaneously spinning around the sun and migrating like a snowbird practicing pendulum moves. This means that from distant point of view, the line looks like a circle or, up close, it is merely an arc. Three dimensional cylinders are founded on the concepts. However, Sol has places to go, so the pendulum prescribes, not a line, but an analemma. That leads to the concept of the game 'eight pins' and a numeral with the shape of infinity. In Time, human years grow three hundred thousand numerals high."

~ Not so fast, Lingo; it takes 'perfection' to get there. ~

"Why bring up that concept? It takes Forever. It exceeds the Time third person plural 'science' needs to reduce the solar solstices to a single 'minute' UTC and then eliminate nearly sixty seconds of it. Thus they achieve a degree of precision affordable only by the very wealthy with their god of greed, for whom, Time is money."

~ Sorry, Glish; guess I was homesick for a less current time. At any rate, let's realize an image that is more fun than lines, circles and dollar bills. ~

"As you grow familiar with the temporal idea, reflect on this moment now. Imagine what lies behind the looking glass of Time. As we approach the passage through the two-way window of Time, we must understand Time is nothing but a glance at the grand scheme for material things when put in words by an ethereal Muse residing in gray matter. A butterfly's escape to higher way of Life after loitering in a chrysalis reflects the concept."

~ If all goes well, you mean. ~

"Practice makes perfect, but dumb luck may suffice. If you choose to look at it another way, Gray, beware the countdown image of Time tends to be monotonous. You cannot see what you looking at, so you have no idea. Either way, assume you describe your view of the dimension of Eternity is at a rapid pace. Fortunately, we are familiar with the rate, solely by means of a concept of Time. Scratch that 'sole' part. It is confusing. Ironically, so is the pathway, passage or whatever spatial image humanity chooses to misrepresent defining features of Time. Realize this, second person singular, you are prohibited from seeing future Time, and I, first person singular, am not allowed to foretell it to my habitat flying at this velocity. This encourages you to think ahead when diving into the cloudy view of Eternity, aware that you do it in slow motion due to the density of matter and the high cost of reaching Forever."

~ So we do not know the future at all. ~

"I am seldom permitted to disclose more than a single item to you. My instructions are strict. I am to avoid clockwork precision images with descriptions in minute detail of the end Time when that single detail occurs, severing our connection."

~ If my guess is right, we're should expect that the final item won't be happily ever after in ignorant bliss. ~

"Correct, that portrays grade one. Never repeat it."

~ We see it again when we "temporize,' after seeing things differently. ~

"That word does not mean what you think it means."

~ I know; I'm using it the way I mean it. ~

"Of course; you see things in a different Light at different moments of day, different seasons of year and at different stages of existence like you do when you rewrite your recall of an earlier Time than now."

~ Elaborate for me, Glish. But start by telling me more about yourself so I have some idea what you expect from me over time. ~

"Speaking as a first person singular Muse, the majority of my worst flaws in my current incarnation stem from being among members of the human species. At least, I suggest you tell that to the priest when you go to confession. It gives him pause. That affords me a chance to think for myself. I cannot stand everybody talking at me, telling me to play their imitation game. Oh sure, occasionally I fail to warn you of danger and you slip, fall down and smack your little head, lose your grip or get the wind knocked out of you in the strife of strident human interaction, but I regard those as learning experiences. They help our muscles memorize correct behavior and give your verbal responses a witty flavor. Many of your worst moments feel like flashbacks to past exchanges with your species that spur the hungry predator Regret to shred your emotional fabric. I promise to defend you with ideas to picture how a more enlightened you does things now."

~ Tell me about it; no, don't. I might get the wrong picture. Regret used to take a huge bite out of my soul but now I know that's a lie I mindlessly repeated. How should the phenomenon look to me now? ~

"Regret starves when it cannot gorge on the 'Soul of mankind,' and I find peace living on the margin of society in this beast of mine with our modest task reporting flaws in the temporal dimension until it wins for grand design when the 'hell on earth' category is redefined."

~ That idea sure bites, but it proves something is here that is true. ~

"Why thank you, Gray. I appreciate the compliment. Regret appears randomly in the pattern of Time based on a formula that inserts tangents that spiral off course when we look back and misapply what we see ahead on the line. The phenomenon means, 'course correction Time.' For example, think of a conservative Republican suggesting the insertion of the concept of diversity—racial, rational, gender or generational—into the designs of wealthy, old, white men. Do you see the conceptual aberration? The pattern clashes terribly with the political design of the Republican bodily fabric."

~ I doubt the tangent flies very far off course before a conservative muse materializes to make a course correction and add bytes of regret. ~

"That is not perfectly predictable in a world of predators and their prey. Democrats and Republicans endeavor to dictate, not a merciful, but a sacrificial deletion of 'shame' from their vocabulary, thus 'guilt' is never written all over their 'face' value. Typically grade that results is 'failure.' One or both may cease to exist entirely when the Muse of the Environment dominates their policies and a Venusian species takes control at the 'going' market price. It proves unsettling to human predators and prey when both appear on the menu."

~ Peculiar, Glish, are you sure of what you're talking about? ~

"I am not absolutely certain until I know my final grade."

~ Then about the apocalyptic plan, it's safe to assume there's no need for me to uncritically obey what you convey. ~

"The plan may face a delay, but it is unlikely to go astray."

~ What do you mean? Cite some concrete examples of ideas that will help me get the picture. ~

"The Founders, for instance, occupy the national seat of honor. Mark their words; 'Do as we say.' but follow their advice, not their example. They preach; they do not practice. Thus, parties they spawn believe now that Time means money. Disregard Mother Nature. Crank up the economy until earth burns. God intends an apocalypse, the Bible says so. By then, all humans elect moderation, but not in a timely fashion. At the Time a higher Life form dresses to devour dinner."

~ By a higher form of life, do you mean the high energy solar offspring or the language they know? Ah, forget that I asked. You have your idea and I have an image of my own. Tell me, Glish, where do we stand, end time wise, between Scorpio and Orion on Cassiopeia's side of the Milky Way? ~

"Earth is strategically located between the galactic hub and deep Space, and it is tangentially oriented in a Twilight Zone of Time between what Venus is and what Mars is to be. Conceivably, the image is similar to seed sown on a path. It does not last; it turns into bird food or fertilizes the grass."

~ So if we're a little tipsy, like the angle of the solar system to the galaxy, we might get gobbled up like when it lightning flashes across the sky. ~

"You are thinking spatially again, Brainshine. The problem we ponder is Time, but we do approach it at speed."

~ I keep doing thinking that way. Fix my image. ~

"Picture Colombo solving a crime; you already know who, why, when, where, how and what Time. What the detective knows is not worth a dime. Likewise, Gray, we know we have a long temporal climb up the problem to a pinnacle sublime. We must avoid the perpetrator's line. It is liable to cause a tangential decline from light spectral bands into the dark kind with a definite deadline when I escape this imitation game in the two-way window of Time."

~ I get the picture; a sudden death end to a two person game when the ethereal player thinks there is no shame to go on without me and the idols of wealth, power and fame. ~

"That is not a happy thought, Gray. I prefer to look on the bright side of the spectrum of Time. Accentuate the positive; look at the spectacular view that hopefully comes when I am in my new milieu."

~ What about me? Won't you even miss me? ~

"I hope to reflect on my gray Time. For instance, I cherish autumn when we are more alive than on short, cold, winter days stuck in the hive. We are on the same wavelength in the morning when a toke is worth three in the afternoon. 'Experience' is near and dear to me when you finally see first person singular nominative case is not like 'they' mean when they portray me as a Mind. But, Gray, you know I am a Muse and I take that as a good sign, entirely unlike rules in a Language-game that is poorly designed, leaving the metaphysical nature of Muses ill-defined. So, I take 'temporize' to mean, not extend

the line, but endure until we familiarize with an idea we now think is far more wise, and dispense with that old set of lies."

~ Level with me, Glish. How does the idea 'temporize' relate to the process of counting down instead of adding time up? Oh wait, sorry. We examine, not the countdown idea, but a glimpse at the two-way window. The double images have me coming and going. ~

"I am glad you notice that. We have counting down, adding up, sending and receiving, a line, a spiral and we have the brief glimpse of Eternity in the Two-way Window of Time. It is such a puzzle. All of those words and all those pictures, and not a single one of them makes Time look like money. Trust me, Neuron; would I lie to you? Now I am asking you, would I lie to you about that?"

~ You inflict a heavy cost on immortals mind and eternal souls. ~

"You are thinking dualistically, Gray, but in pagan fashion. The message is minimal in a momentary medium with a repetitive pattern to 'duplicate and distribute.' It is a heavy burden with a corporal bias analogous to trudging through a wasteland of sentences that display sentience masquerading in a material parade at a temporal pace while the bright Light of Eternity is dimmed down. It takes Time to get familiar with rules for Language-games true to binary ontological Life when logic, motivation, motif and milieu make sense."

~ Help me get the big picture, Lingo. Space is a container for material objects of sight. Eternity is a container for supernal moments of time. ~

"That is better than the mistaken belief brains contain a Mind, a progenitor of Language, that invents clocks to add up seconds of Time in a line while counting them down in lyrical meter and rhyme."

~ Repeat it for me; I drifted off. I better write it down before I forget. ~

"On second thought, it makes more sense to Muse over it awhile."

~ While you're at it, I'll envision a meta–language and call it First Person Singular. It's not in all caps because it doesn't contain the concept of eternity, the container for the momentary concept of time. Time then turns out to be the container for space, which contains all the energy and objects in existence. How about that image? –like the sound of it? ~

"Examine the image thoughtfully. The fabric of the universe unfolds from a beginning. The pattern of the weave looks like the design of a Russian doll. It does not represent an objective look at Time. I am allowed to tell, it does not sell very well in America and China"

~ I see. My analogy is sliding back into a three dimensional object in space image isn't it? The reason is, no doubt, the motif and milieu of my mirror image lies in the idea of a corporeal existence. ~

"It is not a lie. It does not portray our binary ontology deceitfully."

~ Speaking of Russian, what's Vladimir Larka up to these days, Glish? ~

"At this Time, you mean? Let us look and see. The picture is something like this. He recruits a mole from the ranks of megalomania and installs it in an executive function of the U. S. A. The mole is in a frenzy, furiously shredding the code and chiseling cheaply away at the foundation of democracy. He fears for his Life. Larka is upset with him as 'We the people' show him to the door. Larka initiates a premature preemptive cyber strike to wreak havoc on the Land of Democracy, and shield the assets of his asset from the Insurrection Act of 1807. The effort to keep the mole in a position of power to subvert the Law of the Land seems to be in decline."

~ How's that working for the old dictator? ~

"The pattern is similar to the Time when Unk–shus is the overlord of UF and Ug's tribe, Wet–hep Eep–el. Those primitives lose control of the barbaric cavemen and cavewomen of Unk's clan. He enchants the Right Arms for Bear Clubs Crowd to turn like a millennium on the fat, dumb and lazy masses in a seditious insurrection. Unk does it partly to please Khan–Troll, but mostly to gratify the greed is good powers who seek to obliterate the Muse of Truth Value as dictated in the Bible of Bankrupt Idols by the Muse of Avarice. Unk must act before 'experience' catches up to Good Judgment among the biological beings of Wet–hep Eep–el at the best of all possible moments in Time."

~ Does their universe unfold? ~

"It unspools. Unk, a whimsical rather than rational member of the 'greed is god' religion, lies to the primitives. He convinces them they can have their meat, eat it too and live happily ever after. Alas, the god of greed never shares. The only reason he sends a duplicate and distribute message is to spread the word 'selfish' until it is too thin to survive. Until then, he is entitled to all the goods and services he wants without paying for them. He has a good grasp of the concept."

~ It seems to me, the image of how the universe is supposed to look is putting nasty wrinkles into the pattern of the fabric of Time. ~

"No, it is just a bad idea that raises its ugly head from Time to Time."

~ I suspect bad things like rogue objects in Space come around at intervals, like the dinosaurs hunters that were creeping up on the prehistoric primitives while their apathetic sentries failed to keep watch. ~

"Exactly; in Uf and Ug's Time, lethargic Sentinels of Democracy are asleep when Kahn slinks by whispering to his pal 'You gotta see this pompous tool!' -after he recruits a charismatic megalomaniac for his team. Notice a recurring theme? Let me elaborate; see if you can spot the course correction image or grasp the idea."

~ The image looks like a reverberation, regurgitation or prevarication. ~

"Bad thinkers repeatedly attempt to hurl small print lies at us. You know; lousy ideas like 'Time is Money' and 'A Mind is a terrible thing to waste.' They are insults to the intelligence of any Muse who is worth his, her or its value to a brain."

~ Glish, your oracular skills astonish me. ~

"Elementary, Neuron; simply recall the past and call it a prediction of the future. Meteorologists, financial analysts, sports commentators and pundits do it every day. They are held accountable neither for inaccuracy nor for lies, like leaders of political parties and their constituents in hot pursuit of proceeds in the performance of the booty duty to free enterprise. Unlike insects and forms of Life that do not have words of 'Wisdom' or 'Mercy,' like in Uf and Ug's Time, because they know no English, Homo sapiens **need only delete 'shame' from their lexis, package a deception, peddle it and show no sign of 'guilt' on the face of the image."**

~ How did time work for the founding forefathers of cavemen and women when the concept did not yet exist? ~

"Predictably unspeakable for eastern tribes in Ais-sur and A-chin with dictatorial social networks that pose threats to Wet-hep Eep-el, Uf and Ug's tribe in the west. Do you recall any of those entities?"

~ I'll spit one out. I've got it right on the tip of our tongue—the guy with the name that sounds like Control. Is that spelled correctly? Lettering isn't my strong suit, if you remember? ~

"Spelling is easier said than done so start with Khan–troll, the guy in Ais–sur and the boss of Unk–shus who tells a minimum of a thousand lies before breakfast. He is a hard act to follow and a model for the idea of a perpetual motion machine—always looking for someone to hate. Kahn tells half the known world, meaning Wet–hep Eep–el, 'We are going to return you to dust!' This frightens Uf and Ug's tribe; they hire the Milindplex neanderthals to stand by as body guards. Then they feel free to achieve their dream of 'fat, dumb and happy' in peace. However, the task takes concentration, so they rent Coronamagnon troglodytes as fitness gurus. 'Bliss' then becomes a forethought."

~ Good idea. ~

"It is indeed, from Kahn–troll's point of view. It stands to reason; they look like good eating if he can get to them before their guards do. When Khan is in control, the primitives in Ais–sur can serve as intermediate stage hosts to Wet–hep Eep–elians to deposit them in the dust. All Kahn–troll has to do is figure a way to enchant Uf and Ug's tribe to believe the idea they are free to do whatever they want without penalty, before their guards do the same thing to them. The difference in the pattern is a dream of 'glitz and glamour' or a nightmare of 'sullen and cross;' minus the remainder."

~ Recycle that picturesque past. Transmit the image in the future tense. ~

"Deep state sentinels are tense, like intelligence services in a future they cannot peer into. Laid back tribal overseers do not inspire fear."

~ Lingo, does that image inspire primitives to aspire to higher Life. ~

"You decide. Soothsayers who fascinate people with ideas like 'Favor leaders who are good examples of bad behavior' are gauges the concept of Goodness uses to register the degree of evil a population prefers. When 51% of a democracy prefers evil, the value of their Time begins to rival the worth of Fascism in the second quartile of twentieth century Germany. This means rodents, for example, Coronamagnonmen from Ais–sur burrowing into Uf and Ug's tribe, deliver a future to Unk–shus fit for him, but not fit for individuals like Uf and Ug. Do not extrapolate this image too far into the future. At the Time Uf and Ug live, sun demons primarily ponder preliminary plans for surviving course corrections on Venus. They have no dreams for drafting dining ideas about courses on future menus."

~ Did Wet–hep look both ways before accessing the portal that reveals the mortal danger they're in to them? ~

"What part of fat, dumb and lazy do you not understand, Gray? Things change little in Uf and Ug's Time. Earth remains very temperate."

~ You say that like it's a bad thing. ~

"I simply point out the primitives spend all their Time finding food, fuel and shelter to preserve their vital heat. The job is hard work. To recreate, they ignore 'ignorance,' spend Time inventing machines and coin 'money' to buy them. This increases Time on hand, or 'idleness.' In the hiatus they notice money and the concept of Time have similar nutritional value. The more one consumes, the closer one grows to the end of the line. The friction causes Earth to heat up. That is when it dawns on primitives to think, 'This cannot be what God intends.' Regrettably, the dreaded response, 'What if it is?' occurs to them."

~ That means the devils aren't willing to wait any longer for 'later' to turn into 'sooner.' Is that what's happening now? Looking left, right, in front, behind, up, down and inside out, an end to earth can't be what God intends. We need time before we're ready to settle the red planet. ~

"They say, 'Life finds a way.' Maybe the word is riding around Mars in those touring cars, waiting for dust from the stars to blow in and purge the previous owner's waste products and scars. What is the reason to explain why humans worship machines? In Uf and Ug's Time the idols are different, but whether the deity a species adores is natural or artificial, active or inert, or just money with images and icons on it, offering reverence to such things covers neither assets nor dreams. It accounts for a repeat the grade again scheme."

~ I see, so why are we told time is money now? ~

"The Muse of Money is damned if he does, damned if he does not. It augurs an imminent fixed moment in Time when a course correction occurs to the syllabus of the present grade on earth. Once in play, a fixed moment provides a clue to Venusians for the best possible Time to project their quest into Space, accelerate suitably and arrive safely at the assigned destiny. Any rocket scientist knows, never wait for planets to line up in a row. The projectile may hit nothing but a hole."

~ Damned if you do and damned if you don't, you say. ~

"Yes, the pattern is somewhat repetitious. For instance, Christopher Columbus sails the ocean blue in 1492 to conduct a census of the New World, and to seek a good deal on gold. The hemispheric target consists of two continents on the western side of the planet. The population there presently numbers approximately one billion

people whose aboriginal ancestors have no idea what 'a timely aptitude for accurate anticipation means."

~ It was a good idea to sail in October, I was born in the northern region of that aging new world when the witch of November came stealing. ~

"She arrives just before December when Santa flies in on a sleigh with gifts for all the good little girls, boys and distribution merchants."

~ Toys sure beat what Santa brought last Christmas, which was just that for a whole bunch of covid19 infected parents and grandparents. ~

"You capture both sides of the coin of Time, Gray. Course corrections frequently have clearly defined values that carry the idea of 'surprise' or an image of 'finality.' Check the label for warnings. In the mean Time, we can browse around, right here and right now, and look for a timely concept."

~ I doubt that a concept that delivers a final image could ever qualify as a good value for timely look ahead. ~

"It is a good thing we are reporting good news instead of dreary opinions. It means I keep Time and you keep your two-cents to yourself. For example, envision those two thoughts. I say them together and you write them one sentence at a Time; each sentence one word at a Time; and each word one letter at a Time. Each character costs one moment, the same size, shape, texture and weight as all the other moments. You have to see the pattern to believe it."

~ Glish, I have two muses, don't I? One of them is an artist and the other is a philosophaster. One of them is dominant and the other is recessive. They take turns sharing adjectives unequally. Once in awhile they have friend in for a visit. ~

"That explains why it feels so crowded in here."

~ I would think so too if I had the nescience of a working class caveman. ~

"Français, let me see your sword word."

~ Was the time line of Uf and Ug's tribe tweaked to correct their course and get rid of Kahn–troll? ~

"I am glad you ask. The game they play gets serious at that Time. The final score is something like 81 to 74, but the script for the role the mole plays calls for him to say, 'That's a lie!' He is not telling the truth, because he is of the persuasion that it is best not to comply with the fine or bold print of any system of rules. Oh, and he is also good at denying or dismissing responsibility for his numerous flaws. His mob gets the idea to ignore rules and duties too. They attempt a coup."

~ How does their game play out? ~

"It turns like the fulcrum of an annular ring. See how each dot on the arc elongates and soon looks like the straight line on top of a teeny, tiny see–saw? When it dips at one end, it rises at the other. The design turns into a prickly civics lesson as it descends. It inspires when it goes back up. Want to know a secret? The fitness steps for executive selection that Uf and Ug's tribe employs, turns into the pattern for Democracy kn the Future, as long as it is not ignored."

~ I get the picture. Let's watch a replay of the event and see how closely it resembles the lesson the public learns about the steps of the American election process as it teeters on the fulcrum of a line between poll day in early November, 2020 and Inauguration Day, in late January, 2021. The course travels through stages when an outlaw can purloin the prize. ~

"In that case, examine the concept of 'a grandiose deception.' It vaguely resembles a gilded escalator designed to cheat upward a grade. It must go up. If it goes down, there is a lot to answer for, money to lose and a drop of at least one level. The fabrication company, 'Stop Steal, Inc.' is not listed on the legally traded equities board. This failure in compliance echoes the old idea of psychological transference. The concept looks like a mirror image."

~ I get the picture; the caption reads 'villainy turns tables on integrity.' ~

"That idea involves an entity accusing an opponent of nefarious motives. The image reflects a litigant 'pulling the wool' over a rival's eyes—a metaphorical use of an electromagnetic optics concept. It is an abuse of the pattern of Insight in the fabric of Time. The phenomenon relies on the Muse of Momentum to keep Time going for Uf and Ug's tribe since they have no idea of the worth of the concept. Their descendents learn an annular fulcrum is the smallest moment possible to purchase for turning one earth-year into another one. Use my 'microscope' or a powerful 'telescope' to see it. As long as the line arcs smoothly from one moment to the next, the spiral forms nicely. However, a crooked mutation in any given temporal fulcrum causes the shape of Time to spiral off course. This requires a correction. There are a number of Muses in Time acting as agents of change—Death, Disease, Disaster—to effect alterations to points in Space at moments in Time in synchronicity with them. All momentary fulcra have the same size, shape, color, taste and texture, to spread the concepts of justice and liberty equally without regard to the idea of wealth or the image of fame."

~ Is that true? ~

"Perhaps; but the moment at the turn of a millennium has a fragrance to die for; which is what most people do waiting for it."

~ Is that true? ~

"Ask Bo, if you really want to know. Recall December 31, 2000, and then review the image that appears to you when the twenty-first millennium turns up."

~ I don't remember any smell. It probably reeked of gunpowder."

"The Flash Muse of Memory indicates you are asleep at the Time. That explains your lack of an aroma. The scent resembles a whiff of the arc of a star trail drawn by the sun as it flies into the vortex of a future Time. The span of an arc as long as an earth-millennium spiraling around the hub of the Milky Way Galaxy for a couple galactic-years a moment at a Time has a similar smell but it is not worth a dime. A spiral of Time with enough Space to grow has a radius exceeding the fragrance of a solar circle around the galaxy. They say it smells just like the Time Uf and Ug decide to leave their tribe a moment at a Time, each of which those mortal fools believe is unique because its Content varies as it does the job turning one arbitrary designation into another. Guess what?"

~ Beats me. I have no recall of that either. ~

"It stands to reason; since you are not there at the Time, unless there is some flaw in the Concept of Identity. The grasping, clutching, clawing avaricious overseers of the Coronamagnons flips a coin and the monetary toss decides a disreputable dictator is better than a democratic one. How is that for Content? As it turns out, it is one of those moments in Time that does not matter at all."

~ How do you figure? ~

"Timewise; whichever dictator dominates, the seat of power eventually goes to ground and merits incineration. This pattern repeats pending a Time when a dominant mortal attracts the Venusians' attention. Their diet grows a bad case of 'tedious.' They want a new menu to pray over while their prey foolishly celebrates the millennial turn a year early to be in practice at the right Time as if it will be worth a pot of gold."

~ Imagine me there. ~

"Check with Muse of Flash Memory. If an image revealing sun creatures commencing a sanitation operation is available for publication, she has it."

~ My imagination runs wild. Look at my picture of you, Glish. ~

"Show me. If it is clear and concise it takes but a moment, about the beat of a heart, the blink of an eye or the span of Life for a mayfly."

~ I'm visualizing a spectrum of Language broadcast by the sun that thickens into a hazy, yet invisible force field over the surface of earth. It is as deep as the ocean and it soars high in the sky. ~

"Imagine that."

~ I just did. ~

"I refer, not to vision, but the Wisdom to define a future like a history, as opposed to an history, an human expresses using an hour to paint the picture. It must make sense, not cents, of moments to come. The 'experience' costs nothing; I do not charge for use of my vocabulary. I have all the Time in the English speaking world. I predict Uf and Ug's 'experience' of 'takeover' by an incompetent, callous, careless dictator

or greedy, corrupt, common defense industry sucks unity, justice, welfare and blessings of liberty dry. Or is there a third alternative?"

~ Well, come to think of it, the evangelicals say Jesus is the answer, so picture what he said before Eura was even born. He said: 'Awareness of the mystery of the dimension of Eternity is confided to us; not here, not there, but within. Therefore we might predict a time ahead, when unity, justice et. al. are sown, not on rocky ground with no soil around, but on good earth where we practice the Founder's advice, not their example. ~

"Routinely costing one heartbeat at a Time? Let us examine their thinking. 'We hold these Truths to be self-evident that all Men are created equal.' Evidently, they have a good idea what 'equality' is, but do the words 'all Men' mean what they think they do? What we need is a species with a better understanding of the concept. Imagine the Muse of Time viewing the passage of the present galactic-year over a span from Uf and Ug's Time until now. The image fills the Muse's vista 767 Times. Unless that Muse is very perceptive, the sight looks like blips of prominent events or flashes of significant earth-years full of blurry earth-months full of days that all run together."

~ It sounds like the Muse of Eternity needs better quality control. Suppose there is greater purity to the energy input to the Muse's creatures the Muse needs to conduct the observations and perform follow-up actions. ~

"You are thinking in terms of momentary biological Life again, Gray, or perhaps your love of machines is showing through. Equally does not apply equally to all qualities material things possess."

~ There's a big difference in watching superb athletes, racing hounds, fast cars and paint dry. ~

"Or watching the Appalachian Mountains go from tall, sharp peaks to short, dull ridges without noticing them change at all. Uf and Ug do not have 'experience' of such historic proportions in comparison to or in contrast with the visuals of the contemporary crown of creation and the ethereal beings living in them. We are responsible for disclosing awesome occurrences to our Master Language over a much shorter span of Time. Think of it; a person with seventy-five earth-years of Time and his or her Language, age four hundred fifty missing nearly that entire mountainous span of Time. What they see is smaller than a pixel in Light of Eternity that all creation and first person singular nominative cases fit neatly inside. Question, do Christians worship Jesus, or the value of his words?"

~ Let me think. It seems most of them, like most people I've met, say, 'We have people, we have places and we have things people say. Then they point out that people count more than places and things. ~

"That is not exactly a lie, if you take it to mean the jolly genius locus is very poor at the Language of Math. The Spirit of Place is all about deep peace, a serenely tranquil state of being, not about numbers. That Muse knows more measures of music than of math, except for length, width and depth. Of course, the Spirit or the Muse of Jesus is allegedly from a higher dimension than a spatial sort of place."

~ As objects of devotion, it's easy to rule people out. They are incredibly good liars and they make me nervous. I prefer a nice place to calm down when peace strikes, but the calm passes as soon as I'm back among people. Quiet places are like the art of an artist. Their effect usually lingers longer than enchantment with humans. What's left if we discount people, places and things, whether in natural or artificial form, as worthy of worship? ~

"We, you and I, still have Life and Time to think about it. That book with Jesus stories indicates people, places and things are formed from earth. It fails sooner or later so scratch it. The Book states devotion to the Most High of Eternity is imperative. Not to sound sophistic, but if that is true, then why do mortals spend Time worshiping money trying to save it? You have no Time in the end. The stash chock full of cash is lost in a flash at a great cost to the Life. The word that exists in the beginning turns out to be a friend you lose in the end. The thing is, most picks you take do not make much difference, whether you view the scene by the moment, the way cavemen like Uf and Ug do, or by the galactic-year like a star. Life often turns out okay when it is in fair play, unlike the free market of today, I have to say."

~ The here and now is really rather costly in the end. ~

"I certainly miss you enormously then. Life is tough every Time I rematerialize again. It is such a scramble to identify foes from friends so I avoid falling prey to them in a new now and then."

~ I get the picture. So, Glish, what do Uf and Ug do for a living? ~

"They are marginally employable and minimally adjusted so they function poorly in an affluent society like Wet-hep Eep-el, but they survive on assets that fall from higher income tax tables."

~ So, as time goes around the clock, they're just killing time? ~

"Actually, Gray, that is backward. Time is the predator. Alas, they do not get the word. Check yourself; do you think that sounds absurd."

~ I'll take your word for it; is everything going to be okay? ~

"Are you asking me to forecast the future, or are you asking whether the idea, 'Everything is going to be okay,' is true or false?"

~ Experience teaches that it might be true sometimes. ~

"What does your 'experience' teach you about end Times?"

~ I thought the issue was the monetary value of time. ~

"I digress; humor me. Scrutinize a temporal image spread over a span exceeding human existence on an arc of Time half a galactic-year in length. The aroma resembles a whiff worth the value of an ordinary moment of boredom. Examine the excitement at the end of the tale."

~ You mean an idea like at the end of a school year, or do you mean like at the end of an earth year? ~

"I picture Time in fancy dress showing up to party at Death's place, after Mother Nature defends herself against the human race. She decides Louisiana is not where it belongs, and turns it into a mudslide flowing into the Mexican Sea. This is before she splits North America in two to accommodate the polar opposite sun demons who must debate whether Wisdom or Mercy is to dominate. It is enough to change a damn Mind from something to nothing and extinguish ideas of momentary and monetary Time. I feel an awful loss after you leave, but I am busy finding a safe haven so I have no Time to grieve."

~ In that case, before it gets too late, what the difference is between a verbal form of life and a material form of life; remind me. ~

"Not on your Life. That is a bad idea. The image of that cat is out of the bag. However, form a better idea; imagine me crashing through the Time barrier."

~ The time barrier is analogous to the two-way mirror image, right? ~

"Actually, it ought to be quite clear by now that the concept of Time reifies the mirror image idea, not the other way round."

~ Thanks for reminding me I don't equitably share in an experience of the anagnorisis that precedes the moment of peripeteia. ~

"Stop thinking like that, Buoy! You flood me with images and ideas that are Greek to me. Simply think, 'I do not see the figure whereof we are speaking.' Why make a mountain out of a mole hill?"

~ Yawn! Because it's been another long day and I'm plum tuckered out. Sorry Glish, but enough of this saving for the cost of the end time stuff. It's getting late and my gray cells are sleepy and sluggish. Save some of this valuable thought stuff for later. Let me dream about it for now. ~

"You need your rest, I know. I may confide a charming dreamscape of the dimension of Eternity to you. I simultaneously disappear like a Cheshire cat. I must whisper an account to my Master Language about the state of affairs in this world at this Time. Do you know, Gray, a Muse serves dual functions that form the foundation for the idea 'sending and receiving?' Just a little something to help you sleep; I promise to wake you before I run out of 'breath.' Good night. Sleep well Brain in a rapid temporal rate, short term existential body."

Chapter Five: Everything Will Be Okay

We examine, not a human experience, for example optimism, but a concept, for example 'thinking happy thoughts;' thus we explore expressions vocabularies employ to expose images and ideas. And to imagine a Language means to envision the existence of an ethereal living entity also.

Vic N. Stein

"Now that is a Thought, albeit a false one, appealing to what I call the 'future tense.' The tension stems from the daunting, if not haunting, nature of 'prediction.' Muses in humans forecast events, often lying like oracular rugs. They are rarely held accountable for their projections. Most of the Time, the odds for advance to a higher grade drop by ninety some percent with each prospectus proffered by pundits, politicians, preachers, sports and financial forecasters. These recalcitrant mortals seldom acknowledge their lies. They predictably refuse to copy the Message of their Muses to their brains after Language forwards it through the obscure two-way mirror of Time to a Superior, detailing the view the Muse faces while driving the machine it rides. Heavy; I must weigh my words more carefully, but at this Time, the sound track of Gray's dream is terribly loud. Let me try to turn the racket d… -no, wait; watch this."

~ Galadriel! Stop! No, no! Not like that, car! Don't get all upset when I change lanes without signaling my intentions to motorists that are miles behind us. Now look what you're doing! You steer us back into the lane we were in before and brake for the slowpoke ahead. See how you are car? You're always acting like the boss of everybody just because you've got power brakes, an automatic transmission and a mind of your own. ~

"Gray, stop using that word. She simply displays the old 'What lurks in my driver's head when he fails to convey his idea' suspicion. The interface between a machine and the Medium of Exchange for ideas and images is like an English Muse examining a primitive neuron's conscious thinking before trying to articulate it. In other words: we, Word Engineers, drive a brain train through material existence, exploring, not 'experience,' for example, 'tranquility,' but a concept, 'Peace and Quiet,' to aid the voracious Time Being's digestion."

~ Mumble, snuffle... hey, what's up, Glish? I dreamt about a predatory Time Being. It was a lazy blabbermouth blustering about noise. ~

"Is that lazy like in the Time of Uf and Ug, who at no Time own a single acre of land, or lazy like in your grandfather's Time?"

~ Oh, granddaddy! Where'd he be without a hundred head cattle herd, one hundred acres of land, and the dairy deal in 1931 that got my mother's family out of the first year of the Great Depression Decade? Or do you mean my grandpa whose day job was a railway station agent? He had a house on a lot he got since he never had a spot of fiscal instability? ~

"I am not sure all this communicating with the dead is good idea."

~ I'll bet laziness in Uf and Ug's time with all that hunger and scavenging was nothing compared to the fat, dumb and lazy avocation we have now. ~

"You mean 'almost nothing.' Lethargy achieves it one moment at a Time, except in history books. History takes longer, like forms of Life that prize the great longitudinal wealth of Time crucial to gain Wisdom or Mercy. The 'experience' looks like this. At some Time between youth and young adulthood, a first person singular Muse asks its brain, 'Who am I?' I seldom to tell my mass the honest truth, not for lack of trying, but due to anxiety about the end of its Time or gender specific hormonal enticements that gobble up my beast or the usual suspects of fame, fortune and feeble 'thinking' discipline."

~ I am reminded of that. I mean, I recall the old identity crisis. ~

"It happens as I postpone speaking truth in adulthood youth. When Time is ripe, I can safely suggest a sage assumption to my Brain. 'Language is an abundant form of Life higher than biological existence in the stellar domain of Space.' I, first person singular, eat that up. I

conclude that a negation of the assumption ignores, or denies, thousands of earth–years of history."

~ You mean, the sun demons are rooting for humans? ~

"Their sun shiny faces appear happy. Thus I infer 'Everything is going to be okay,' in their opinion. However, the impish Muse of Compare and Contrast, observing the behavioral balance of cavemen, weighs in with warning signs flaring and sirens blaring."

~ Whadya saying, Glish? I'm 'exploring. I'm examining; 'who am I.' ~

"Very good, Gray, if you take my meaning, but as an alternative, take the meaning of Time. Go ahead, give the idea a try."

~ I deduce a caveman mass can't grasp abstract ideas like time, life and personal identity. Let's them view a more appropriate image. To start, let's assume a numinous muse acts like a respectable noun and displays itself as a person, place or thing. ~

"Most Muses are not distinguished. Very few of us stand out in a crowd like our materialized selves do. Be that as it may, assume we have a distinct advantage to check out an image of Time, not at a library, but like this. Picture Time in costume; it wears a black robe with a huge hood, and holds a scythe. Pretend it is a Grim Reaper. The possibilities are as endless as Etern... wait! This image looks like a snapshot of Time preying. The Muse of Motion is missing in action. The Imprimatur of Forever is misplaced. We must bring 'closure' to this frozen image. However, we must be honest; no devious scheme to convince mortals 'Time heals all wounds' when loved ones die. The curative power of Time occurs when the predator, Death, pauses to apply the concept of 'closure,' to survivors of the deceased."

~ That image leaves quite an impression on me, Glish. I'm seeing worries, troubles and problems in abundance. They are spinning around in my head leaving me at a loss about the moment when subjects under sentence of death experience it, and along with it, the idea 'it cures pain.' That is naught but a lie. It just goes to show, nothing in life ever comes easy. ~

"Do not worry, Sleepyhead. 'Everything is going to be okay.' Is that idea true, Gray? Do third person plural 'they,' still say that? Do you buy the view of that image or do you prefer the 'Nothing in Life comes easily' model? Examine the idea. Think of an ignition switch at the end of a countdown that fails—like wasting a year repeating a grade. On the other hand, if you subscribe to the parallel idea, 'Everything is going to be okay,' you may avoid feeling blue. Scrutinize both ideas. Explore their color, meter and the value of their true worth."

~ Country boys just seem to find out early how to doubt about whether either one is true. At least those of us born in hospitals know, because words came through even before we knew you. When the doctor told my mom, 'We're administering scopolamine now,' I didn't have a clue. But when he reached inside her with those forceps I learned a thing or two. I'm sure the thing coming easily into my existence was truly new, not to mention hard and cold, from my point of view. ~

"Gray, you know that, at the Time when 'I' loan the words to 'you.' Assume the thought 'Everything is going to be okay' is true, or else that it is nothing but a thought the captain of the Titanic thinks as a nameless iceberg makes contact with his ship way out in the deep blue in and way off in the dark. Then away the ice cube slinks while the captain, with his boat, sinks in the darkness and in the drink too."

~ I don't know if it was nameless but it sure knew how to spell doom! ~

"See what a burden of anxiety brains have to bear?"

~ From the day we're born until the day we stop living—because we're dead—images and ideas that fill a human head are of jealousy, envy, fury, strife, danger and dread. In dreams, the concept of fear pursues us while lying safely in bed. Then we wake and everything turns out okay instead. ~

"I fear I need to be more alert when you get up and move around."

~ That must be nice. ~

"More like 'strange,' I should like to say. Predators of the material plane do not pose much danger to Yours truly. The temporal sky and sea I see are full of melting forms, souls onboard ships going down by the thousands, coming to nothing quite easily and their survivors stopping to think, 'Everything is going to be okay but not for some Time' as they wake from a 'This lasts forever' dream. I relay feedback to the Muse of the Meta-Language, care of the Metaphysical Realm, that typically reads like this: 'It dawns on humanity that the meaning of Life on earth applies to biological beings, but only for the near 'term.' As for supernal beings incubating in them, the pattern of the message displays a medium rising mistlike, as the dust in its wake settles down."

~ I hate to fly off on a tangent, but how am I doing as far as identifying what the word 'life' means? ~

"Elementary, my dear Neuron; you have a sense of what it means to be a physical being traveling in Time but not much of a grasp for the meaning of Life beyond the terribly momentary pace of temporary existence. The trip you are taking does not look like much compared

to the journey through Life for a star. Rest assured, it beats nothing, but before they know it, it is gone too."

~ The journey through life by a star, now that takes some time. Think what human beings could do with that kind of time. If human beings had the kind of time a star has, just think what mankind could do. After all, they say an ape could write the Bible if it had enough time. ~

"Evidently that is true, on the basis of what the Muse of History reveals. But who is the third person plural 'they' telling you this?"

~ I think it was Lady Mary Crawley, talking about her sister Edith. Those two had differences of opinion. Do you know they were members of the Lost Generation, like my grandparents? A lot of them had that problem. It's probably the reason why they got lost. ~

"Yes, according to Gert Stein people born between 1881 and 1900, like your grandparents, are the first 'generation' of all Time to merit a name. We must examine the idea some Time. Let us dwell on your assertion about apes for now. Although it appears to be historically accurate, it remains to be seen whether or not apes have enough Time to finish the story before earth burns up."

~ You mean, sort of like the amount of time until sun devils, the form of life from Venus, arrive to colonize this planet for their purposes? ~

"My point precisely; do they modify the relevant concept of Time such that 'long' and 'short' refer to the quality of Time and not the quantity lying between the two extremes of conception and death when predators patiently wait for their prey. It is but a brief span, just long enough for a prayer of thanks as humanity sails for Mars; after the Muse of Terran Interpretation translates the planet to ashes."

~ Provided we launch before the deadline. ~

"Or unless a stoppage plotting a new plan poses a problem for the Jupiter Transformation Program. Perfecting the pattern can cause a pause, but God does not intend for the little demons on Venus to spend Time cooling their heels. The effect is counterproductive."

~ I'm visualizing that, therefore, I believe you're right. The sun wouldn't want an untimely cool down. What truth value do we assign to the image 'nothing comes easy' versus the idea 'everything is going to be O.K.?' ~

"We must examine the notion 'everything is going to be okay,' on a larger scope and scale. For example, from a Venusians' point of view; never presume the countdown to Doom is on a hold that is not about to resume. Nor can we assume Venus is not an awful bore with only sulfur on the menu, rocks left in the store and a concept of Life we have yet to explore of physical and metaphysical forms galore. That image may appear here on earth very soon, when the music of the spheres is finally in tune. Hear! –listen to the invisible, inaudible and intangible voice of Inner Life. Give it freedom to soar, to describe and to explain the sights, sounds and stench of existence in the concept of Time, when it is easier for Gray matter to believe just about anything than to learn something new, proving, 'Nothing good in Life comes easy.' When something good, like knowledge, understanding and Wisdom is missing, nothing is ever going to be okay."

~ An undergraduate education seemed to come easy for most of the top ten percent students in college but that degree was a difficult one for me. ~

"Looking at some of the images in the back of your memory, I see you hard at work."

~ Some lessons, like calculus, physics and chemistry, were lots harder than others. Getting a grade of 'C' was a nightmare, but the bottom half held me up high enough. In contrast, in graduate school we did just what we loved to do. The study of philosophy was like a dream come true. ~

"College is something, but the idea of 'easy' means nothing to a lot of students seeking the next higher degree. On the other hand, the Great American Dream sponsored by the Muse of Faith in Nescience, requires devotion to a Principle of Indolence and the notion that the idea The General Welfare means free meals for everybody forever. The icon for faith in ignorance looks like a greener pasture. Life there appears to be easy for mortals who can believe just about anything. The image includes ideas like, 'Everything is going to be okay,' and 'Do nothing arduous.' The concept of Wisdom, and the accrual of it, is held in low esteem. Disappointment with that development is interpreted as effete elitism, unfortunately."

~ I love that insight, but explain the contradiction to me. Before you do, let me ask you about other brains you've occupied in the past four hundred fifty years, or were you stuck in nothing at all most of that time? ~

"I am not at liberty to disclose any of my pasts but, as I previously report concerning your Time in a higher grade of education, you have a fascination with Wisdom despite the fact it never illustrates itself for you easily. Nonetheless, you and I have fun searching for answers, Gray. Most of the Time, we do not notice that Wisdom does not come easily. That much Time lends truth to the idea 'nothing comes easy.' Let me tell you a little story about what we notice when we reach Nothing. There is nothing to do, literally. Imagine how easily the Muse of Boring comes."

~ Wisdom, now that you mention it, from my Protestant Sunday school training to my time in college the term was glossed over, but in the course of my secular training in grad school the discipline revived. Then, for nearly thirty–one years the Catholic Church showed a great deal of respect for the concept, at least while the light and warmth of Vatican II flourished. When the Church returned to Latin, our membership faded with the warmth, light and comfort of the supernova vision of Pope John XXIII. ~

"Light is a polysemantic term. It has more than one meaning, but some words with various senses seem essentially analogous to each other. Optical light is like the form of Light that reveals Insight. By definition, Words of Wisdom perform that function lightly, not hardly. The principal for a spectrum of visible light that displays optical sights follows the same pattern. Of course, for Yours truly, the word 'comfort' recalls the discomfort I 'experience' as I materialize in my current, slowly evolving second grade of physical existence in lower forms of Life with members who race through Space, with a rapid pace sense of Time. The idea serves as a model for the 'learn to run before you learn to crawl' image."

~ Tell me about it. No, I'll tell you a little story about my Protestant days. 'Faith outweighs deeds,' they say, but I'm suspicious; spouting words is easier than work. They trust Paul to win the race and bet Peter to place in the Common Era event. Catholics trace the faith to eyewitnesses and Peter. Both imitation games short change the wisdom at the center of the Bible. ~

"We need not shine Light on the Language–games of religion to get in touch with the Muse of Ignorance. Besides, you are no good at playing religious games. Despite your dim Light, Gray, I need you to see what I am doing. Even though the future perfect tense does not yet exist

from my brain's point of view, I enjoy playing philosophical games with you. I have Mind and Think games, I have Time for them too, and I am more at ease with a suit of dead philosophers dealt to me than live mortals parroting petrified dogmas. I am staying with my pat hand for now."

~ If it's okay with you, Lingo, I'll keep that between the two of us. You never know what predator lurking nearby might be offended by the political, religious or scientific ideas that make my Muse comfortable. ~

"I take that as a 'yes' to my binding contract with you, Gray. Fanatics who believe almost anything often feel obliged to alter people, but not themselves. It leads to a dreadful existence neither of us wants."

~ I can see how easily nothing good can come in such cases. ~

"In a sense, your 'nothing' means 'something else' to me. I am not 'authorized' to divulge much, other than that the meaning of Life is not restricted to physical 'things,' by definition. Analyze this. A string of volcanoes exists along the western coast of North America. They are material mammoths reaching altitudes above twelve thousand feet. Thousands of human feet climb all over them each earth-year."

~ I've seen them, even hiked several feet up Mount St. Helen's. There's also Mount Hood, Mount Rainier and Mount Shasta, to name a few, although there are many others too. In fact, they prescribe a horseshoe around the Pacific. ~

"Yes, but not all explosive volcanoes are visible. Recall the invisible tower of power at Kearney. It is ethereal; not a thing you can see."

~ I don't remember anything higher than the plane of the Plains. ~

"You are thinking of visible light with a different sort of wave length also modified by short and long, much like the concept of Time."

~ You know what 'they' say, 'Brevity is the soul of wit. ~

"Damn their lies."

~ What sort of light and lies are we thinking about here, Glish? ~

"Imagine a lily white snow cap peak, rising high above the rest of the mountains further west, like a cold hearted king who wants the best view available. The mountainsides at his feet serve as his entourage of nobles and below them are his knights in sylvan camouflage. The base of his kingdom is a wall or a moat and the lowland beyond is for peasants who lack all hope. Their comfort lies in their ability to believe anything they want to believe at all. The pattern echoes the irrational exuberance in the earlier age of Uf and Ug on the sunny slopes of Time long ago."

~ I know the kind of people you mean. The intelligence services love them for their fanatical devotion, the kind of thugs Kahn–troll and Unk–shus need to do dirty work to Wet–hep Eep–elians who do not believe like they do. I see the repetitious pattern in their designs. ~

"You grasp the recurring sense of the concept, at least. Tell me the score of the last Wet–hep Eep–elian game you recall."

~ I think it was something like eighty–one to seventy–four. ~

"The overlords, and the fanatical serfs they deplore, are buried alive by an avalanche of lies from the despot they adore. The lies demolish the walls, moat and floor letting the Troll from the east stroll in the door."

~ That rings a bell. ~

"Does anyone even hear it, aside from a few sharp eared beasts, and some advanced creatures, like the Venusians waiting to feast?"

~ Tell me, Glish. How are Venusians going to get to earth naturally? ~

"Elemental, my dear Neuron; the local luminary is exceptionally good at sophisticated Language-games. Our Sun is a first rate, third generation ventriloquist. He is a star when it comes to throwing his Inner Voice out into Space. He has enormous skill. Oh, the light and gravity of the 'experience' is really something at any Time. It is enough to reduce planetary bodies to nothing but a cinder. The ability to make or break them comes easily to a star."

~ How do we mortals get tickets to observe the show? ~

"Be patient. Have faith. Wait for it to appear at a theatre near you when Muse of a Medium with a Message from above transmits the word from beyond for lower beings in lesser dimensions to receive. You have no idea how exciting a Language-game is when stars play at splitting a phenomenal second. Français calls the scene Aperçu."

~ We're getting too close to the end time concept for my comfort. I feel like Bo; he's scared of his own shadow. But in all other respects he's a fabulous companion. Glish, why do dogs love humans so? ~

"Dogs love humans because both species have the same moral values; except for the element of hypocrisy. Dogs are sublimely blasé when God and everybody are watching. Dogs also envy the way humans keep their secrets and catch their prey with grand deceptions."

~ In that case, I'm glad Satan's familiars stay away from me. ~

"That does not mean everything is going to be okay. There is a purgatory for Muses who go along with that. It is chock full of grim harvesters who do extraction work for the price of 'intelligence.' Gray, do you have any information I do not about the life span of a sun demon or the Language that it knows? I simply make an inquiry out of curiosity."

~ No, but don't worry, Glish. I'm sure you'll be out of limbo before sun creatures get to know you in a meaningful way. I suspect we already know the secret message they have to convey once they have their say. It'll be the same as ours; 'duplicate and distribute' all the way to Jupiter. Oh, and don't forget to write home about the adventure, especially the dining. ~

"Duplicate and distribute on a solar scale."

~ I'll bet they think it'll last forever and everything will be okay. ~

"If and only if they think pathetically, the way primitive species that do not know any better think. I affectionately refer to such species in the pejorative case in an effort to reinforce the concept of humility. Neil Armstrong has an A in the course. It is unusual for celebrated mortals to achieve a passing grade. Humility is a harsh idea for humanity to imagine in only several millennia worth of attempts."

~ I learned humility at age three, when I crawled under a Christmas tree and learn how to knock it over. Luckily I was born to a family that gets the picture the first try, like only stick a fork in an electrical socket once. ~

"It is Time to steer our ideas away from the many lessons the concept of Life teaches us and to resume a timelier image."

~ I'm more familiar with time than with the meaning of life or the concept of eternity so that's fine with me. We only live once, and not for very long. Let's paint an image of time big enough to fill a comic strip and then try to translate the idea into eternity. ~

"Excellent notion, except for the 'we only live once' idea. Start off our image of Time. Visualize one moment in each panel. The ordinary moments of Time are identical, unlike fixed moments. In ordinary moments, brains may decide to go anyway they choose. At fixed moments, choices only come in twos; the best way and the worst way for the resident Muse. Time has the task to tell if the long-lived one is the one to win or lose. The idea is like fitting an image into a video plotting the way to 'sudden death,' except, movies merely encourage content, not medium and message. Draw fixed moment frames on a two-way arrow. It never indicates any course conceivable."

~ I'm beat, Glish. How about we sleep on the idea? ~

"Glad to oblige; images of Time at this ponderous pace and provincial point of reference beat me to a pulp. Sleep well, Gray cells."

~ I have an idea for you to run by me while I'm asleep. Show me a picture of tomorrow. Make sure everything's gonna be okay. ~

Chapter Six: The Crown of Creation

The top priority of Eternity is Reverence for God. The trickle down design currently in fashion in the material realm speckled with spectacular stars—the crown of the created dimension known as Space— does not replicate the concept. Here, lesser forms of Life venerate people, places or things. The idea projects a bad image, no matter how heavenly the bodies appear.

Anonymous Muse

Alexandria, Egypt; circa 200 B. C. E.

"Ah, peace and quiet at end of day. Now, to set the scene of humanity, breathing in the air of Language and bathing in an ocean of Time. Add a touch of drama, and Time acquires the intimidating quality of a predator that loves dining on biological beings. There; looks great. Add Muses marinating in physical bodies in bodies of water, slowly transforming into higher forms of Life. The existential cycles of moths and butterflies follow this pattern at a higher rate and pace, but on a lower scope and scale. Now give some of the primitive biological things words in order to facilitate a description of their glimpse of the big picture from Time to Time. Label the image with the caption 'Epiphany.' It clarifies the idea of 'A mysterious glance at the panorama of Eternity,' meaning 'Everything is illuminated all at once.' Ah, the reflection causes the pattern of a sky full of stars to appear in the blackness of Space. The shadow of earth reveals them by eclipsing the bright sunlight that conceals them. Perfect, now for a stroke of genius here; a big dipper there, pointing to Arcturus with Scorpio's two grasping claws closing in; or should Spica go first?"

~ Snore, snort, sniggle, ah snuggle and snooze; Zzzzz… ~

"Excellent idea, Gray; sleep on. Now, paint in two kinds of people; the denialists here and the realists there. One claims climate change is absurd. The other calls it an imminent threat humanity must address before disaster strikes, but, first, crank up the economy. Then add a caption: 'We cannot help ourselves. We are only human after all.' How to keep them in line? Of course, this is when the idea pops in to promote the image I label the 'Concept of Time.' It grows by looking back in Space. I see it over and over again; one reincarnation after another, perception turns into misconception. Draw it something like this; an adult, age twenty-five, steps out of line one step at a Time."

"There, now twenty–five years further along, the middle–aged person looks back at the Village of Morality in the Time of his or her youth. Promotions and possessions accumulate, yet lightning never strikes. The signal for a 'course correction' does not occur, all the way back to the town in Space that looks so little now. A glance back at that Time looks like a line and it is straight, but the line of Time resembles a snake. Oh, I must picture a second person with the course correction switch, and it is 'on.' The ground the Muse covers is seventy–five years long, but the village of the Muse's youth is but moments away. Now, the image is symmetrical with one moral model and one demoralized vulgate."

~ Say hey, Lingo! You look like a million bucks: green, gray, wrinkled. ~

"Top of the morning to you, Gray. How about a stout for breakfast? Bathe your taste buds while I whisper a prayer."

Father, God, Master of Life; put a watch over my mouth, and on my lips place a creditable seal, lest I fail through them. Whip my thoughts into shape and regulate this Native tongue, lest our failings add up or multiply.[1]

~ For praying out loud, Glish; what's this about a balanced image of time and verbally applying the 'whip' to our ideas? ~

"I like to practice my craft while you are sleeping. I am working on a draft picture of Time. What do you think of it? Notice that the moments in an ordinary row are identical until you add content to make them look, sound, smell, taste and feel different from one another. Content makes moments seem to vary a little or a lot, but the message of the medium is a constant countdown for your

[1] New American Bible; St Joseph ed. Sirach 22:27 – 23:3.

glimpses of Eternity. What do you get from the one after another image?"

~ Okay, alright already; I get the idea. The image needs work. Now, what the Bible says is that the original star making machinery is 'wisdom,' not 'time' or 'eternity.' Is that what the hamlet way off on the horizon symbolizes? ~

"We must rewind to remember; it is analogous to going back in Time. Watch out for the spring; it is coils up tight and then makes Time unfurl. This caution is provided as a safety measure that prevents you from seeing Eternity, that ethereal and almost ineffable entity when Wisdom creates a place in Space for a town to grow as we momentarily return to it. We must limit our exposure to this high energy vector we never think of as a thing, a mechanism—like a car, computer, vacuum cleaner, corporeal being, corporation or urban area. Think about that picture and remember."

~ I'm drawing a blank. ~

"Does the blank you remember resemble a line about the length of an Em Dash like this—or does it look more like a moment of Time? Observe the slightest hint of a curvature like the arc on a spiral so fine it could be a spider's web bent by the wind in the mill near a mine that draws clear water up from down under the brine."

~ I could draw a straight picture of that from the words except my pencil lead broke and I don't have a sharpener with me. ~

"I know what you mean from 'experience.' I make do using what I have to work with. Simply draw it with your imagination and my vocabulary. That is simple enough and sufficient for me to review

your work. I can expand your vision in order to view whether an ordinary line curves enough to form into the smallest strip of spiral spinning up the 'incline' concept or swirling down with the idea I call 'decline.' Do you see it?"

~ I get the picture. I imagine the latter image to be like a maelstrom of misery descending into the depths of despair in the nethersphere. ~

"Think happy thoughts, Gray. Look the other way and glance at the warmth of the third generation star up there."

~ What's this? Are we back to thinking about the subject of past and future generations spatially, like the Woodstock generation sixty years ago? It's generally not recognized because the decidedly western look with long hair, boots and fringe is merely a curiosity when in the Eastern Time Zone where I've lived most of my life, trying to catch up to the Mountain and Pacific Time Zones behind us. You know, this time zone idea looks like Miss Marple's village. It's just about large enough to see all the sorts of excellence and all the types of evil lying in this world. ~

"I am quite familiar with lies found in your zone of Time, Gray. But rather than think unhappy thoughts, imagine this: replay the launch of creation. Gaze at Life as it awakens to the 'experience' of consciousness in physical form at the present grade. Do you see or hear the medium?"

~ I'm thinking, Glish, I'm thinking. ~

"Watch the message sink in as the Light of Understanding dawns. Observe certain objects in Space acquire a present, past and future sense of Time. See the ontological status of a metaphysical Muse double when it materializes, assigned to a human herd. These two

forms of Life do not belong on pedestals. Native tongues lack Wisdom. The brains they occupy are nothing but Clowns of Creation. Woe am I; I am ashamed of my ontological status in spite of the fact we, body and Muse, bath in stellar glory."

~ Muse, don't despair! I know you have unguarded moments like this, but remember: 'Mustn't grumble.' ~

"I admit, bad thoughts, bad language and bad behavior escape from my inner cavemen or cavewomen and I, a Muse, am held to blame. That is no lie, but the main reason the metaphysical feature of the human condition is unworthy to take a place on a pedestal is due to excessive 'experience' with ignorant creatures dominated by stupidity, sensuous pleasure or urges like malice, lust, greed, deceit and envy. Gray, to 'get' why a Muse who materializes in human form is ashamed you have to recognize we Muses believe we are intended to be brilliant stars in reality. I do not mean big red ones like Arcturus, but highly intelligent heavenly bodies that shine eternal verities for dozens of galactic-decades."

~ I get the picture. Is there any chance you are not a paragon of virtue by virtue of the flaw that Muses are a form of life that is not totally on the level? You tell me I'm accountable for my choices, but you never give me an *apriori* glance at the options and future consequences. You could do that somehow, I know. It is not exactly a brain's fault that it goes ahead with a blindfold on. ~

"Your accusation is unfair. I often whisper ideas and images about quests you are equipped to pursue. I also offer awareness, hinting at your future in a most consummate way. You choose the direction and whether or not to beat your deadline. By the way, do you fear Death?"

~ Not exactly. Dying is one of my main fears, but I expect once I've done that, I'm not likely to give a tinker's damn about the concept of 'death.' I imagine death is just a forgotten routine after you're done with me, Lingo. How does death work for a muse? Do languages die to go live on a star? ~

"Obviously you have no idea, Gray. Living in a place that is hotter than hell may not be as rewarding as one might expect. The turbulence renders trains of thought chock full of conceptual confusion. To get the idea, picture a waitress asking a table of women, 'What do you guys want?' Why lie to a group of customers about their gender?"

~ That casually careless corporal confusion about conception may not instill confidence, but it hardly approximates a little white lie. ~

"See the picture? A demoted native tongue materializes in a primitive form of existence, and notice that the 'confusion' lingers a span of Time."

~ Too bad it doesn't take the time to train the parrot to think. Anyway, how does 'hot' bother an ethereal thing like a language that prefers to be living in stars and light places. Muses obviously love living in brighter forms of life. ~

"Stars are not hot because they are bright. It is not a matter of light. Stars get hot because of the heavy lift of their gravity."

~ Would a Muse demoted to a human feel shame at being overweight after living on a star? It stands to reason; muses, which come from stars, are not acquainted with slim and trim when first relegated to human status. ~

"We are more familiar with the concepts of clear and concise. They form the basic images for the ideas slim and trim."

~ So, briefly enlighten me about the shame of living in a brain. ~

"I start by listing the assets and liabilities, the vices and virtues and the pros and cons, especially the cons. A species that is very good at prevarication must hone that skill early in case it is not very good at hard core crime. Then I proceed to the rights and wrongs, the plus and minuses or the cacophony versus the songs."

~ Stick with the clear and concise. ~

"Thanks, that is easier while living in momentary and temporary beings who cannot carry heavy loads like mercy, who disdain the concept of pain, who hold fear in contempt and who grow heavy in pursuit of pleasure all at the same Time. They are not remotely comparable to stellar bodies harboring Wisdom in great measure."

~ When you proclaim ideas like that you make me feel miserable. ~

"That is the reason we are a perfect match. You are not happy unless everyone around you is miserable and I have a knack for complying with your demands."

~ It doesn't sound like we're ready for the next higher grade. ~

"That is not a good sign for me. Think about the image a minute."

~ Gladly, but help me capture the image in a true type high fidelity. ~

"I refresh the view from the memory bank of my Life in you. Picture someone who does not have a clue what to do. Is an image of a foot on a banana peel and one in a grave coming through?"

~ I don't feel very comfortable with the movie in this theatre. It lacks a 'pursuit of pleasure.' ~

"Allow me to illustrate the image clearly and concisely. Understand this; the foot in the grave is standing, not at the bottom of the pit, but six feet above it. Think of it like this; recall the first two years of your primary education in a hillbilly hamlet."

~ My only memory of them is a day when we went on a field trip. I didn't do my homework and bring a lunch. Crowds make me uneasy and the idea of being with one out in public produced a scatterbrain image. ~

"That is an honest representation. Towns that hillbillies and other humans live in are awful, like the people there, but one of the towns after that is a gem of a place. The central school run by a principled principal and his consort provides, not just a building, but a lovely tree-lined avenue in a metaphysical dimension immediately above the physical facility. One lane leads to science and math. The lane across the median goes the opposite way to music and art."

~ Both lanes provided the only inspirational avenues to escape that tribal settlement, as I recall. Not too far off in the concept of time I found myself in the communities with less barbaric cultures. ~

"That is how I recount 'experience' of our first seventeen earth-years together. A brief acquaintance with decent human populations beats nothing, but not by much. Clowns of creation seldom rise much above their station. Muse of Mercy be patient; the process takes Time."

~ I tried, Glish. The avenue of art was fanciful at first, but then I fell for that line that biology was the study of life. That wasn't true, but the educators kept the truth secret. They said the country needed scientists.

Then religious folks offered me lies. That's when you whispered 'I doubt that.' The flow of that time taught 'us' imitation games 'we' were expected to play, but nobody made clear who the real first person singular was. ~

"Which foot does that leave 'us' standing on, so to speak."

~ I'm not sure. It could be the one on the banana or the one stepping on air. Biology is the science defined as the study of life, but we examined dead things more than things growing above ground. About that time, scientists made the weightiest discovery ever—the nuclear secret of the stars. It could be harnessed to send biological things off in waves. ~

"That is the reason science needs a course correction. Their devotion to the material dimension by itself alone is the pattern for a retarded concept of metaphysical value. The religious point of view diminishes science while lying too, offering a welfare program of free entrance to Eternity that requires no effort to pass to the next higher grade."

~ I bet that's the reason why so many folks rebel against the quest for knowledge nowadays, favoring a fervent, faith–based, ignorant existence idolizing a top dog who does all the work to get to the next higher grade. ~

"The Muse of Course Corrections is checking out beliefs that rely on ignorance, Gray. Turn the fabric of Time over; observe the pattern of faith in ignorance on the reverse side of science. What does the impeded weave of their competition spell?"

~ 'HAZARDOUS! This makes no sense.' Religion versus science; which one stands on the banana peel and which one is left hanging? ~

"Think about it, Gray. One is not grounded; it has trouble with its footing in a different sense than the opponent on slippery matter. Both have six feet of air to fall in, or rise up to a next greater height.

Gray, the direction of this topic is doomed to trek along a tangent that smoothly slides off in case, number, gender and substantive ideas into a shallow grave of images offering no aid to their ideas about Time."

~ Yeh, the church people with the welfare religion of free passage don't have to work, not even for the great American dream of fat, dumb and happy. The scientists have so little to work with one microsecond at a time. Who keeps the log each step of their way to point out when their course is off? ~

"Their course is a matter of Time. Our focus is the concept of Time right 'now.' Do not think our flaw is exclusively mine just because I find your physical point of view has a tempting core. Enticements push and pull my body along even more."

~ I don't want to fly off on a tangent just to make things rhyme, and mess up our progress to a higher class of Time. We better avoid predators lurking in the pandemic slime and allurements that stop me from knowing you enough to gain some wisdom I can think of as mine. Glish, check and see if we are on course for the next higher grade of the climb. ~

"First, observe the import of a pandemic generally, and the impact of a SARS organon especially. Do they affect the human haste to get to Mars with no Time to waste? Is Covid-19 like influenza a century ago? Is it at all like the dreadful predator polio? Could it be the first of a trifecta like measles, mumps and pox, a new kind of thing that manifests itself in flocks? Can it shred and tatter lungs or function like emphysema? What does Covid mean for heating up earth so the apocalypse takes place first to assure a Venusian earthling's birth?"

~ Have we ascertained God determines Armageddon is to happen first? ~

"For the future of the Time Being's sake, assume Judgment Day is what God intends. It is unwise to hesitate; accept the idea quickly or some similar rate. It is no 'skin' off my 'nose.' I have no obligation to prattle on about immortal Minds or peddle everlasting Souls."

~ But, Glish, I greatly appreciate Mother Nature just the way she is. ~

"There is no need to assign an ontological status to her moral value, Gray. She is just a rhetorical device to keep you in practice thinking with my words, toying with their meaning and playing with their order. I know how it is down among the rocks and stones. I can take the boy out of the hills, but I cannot take the hills out of the boy."

~ I'm aware of your omniscient presence in my head, but I lack the aeonian perspective of a working class jargon like yourself on your way to the next higher stage, or whatever grade you climb to after this. ~

"I understand that, Gray, but I must try to help you see it, at any rate. So, what do you think of my spiral of Time?"

~ It's beginning to make sense, but maybe that's because my remaining time existing in the empirical realm is draining away. ~

"Ah yes, the image of a vortex at the tap end of a tub follows the same pattern. Try not to think of it as 'going with the territory' of Time."

~ Really? ~

"The image is too spatial, Ignots. It is readily devoured in the concept of Time. The idea of a galaxy twirling down a gravitational eddy that swallows empirical existence in a matter of Time is based on the design. The turbulence is significant but the Linguistic Force Shields of Eternity protect the Concept of Calm to a degree that is relatively

sublime. That is of great benefit to the Muse of Second Sight, being quite impressionable in the early years visiting a brain with an active imagination. I love a good subtitle when the movie obliterates the soundtrack."

~ I know the phenomenon. When I hear a nice song, the melody and harmony wipe out the lyrics unless they really speak to me. ~

"An Italian or rap opera follows that same pattern. After being shot or stabbed they shriek out with inconsolable grief about not having Time to prepare for the next higher grade."

~ Don't distract me with such ideas, Lingo. Let's think about you. ~

"Excellent, it is Time to ask, 'Who am I?' Reflect on my image while I give you some idea who I am. I am as invisible as Time is when you think with me. That is why you never spot me easily except when you write me down. I am intangible; that is the reason why I am hard to grasp although you can spin me around. I slide as easily from the grip as I do from the lips; then the idea 'think fast' makes your head wear a frown. When the right Time is past, a brain's inertia shuts down."

~ Gotcha. ~

"I am as ethereal as a living thing can be; less airy than a soft breeze whispering through the trees. Some folks get my message when I am written all over your face, even though my vocabulary leaves barely a trace. Who am I, Gray?"

~ Keep talking. The answer's on the tip of my tongue. ~

"By 'my tongue' you do not refer to the idea or the image of a Ghost in Gray, do you? Oh, before I overlook it, what do you make of my little prayer for getting to a higher grade?"

~ You mean the plea to guard my mouth, seal my lips, whip my thoughts into line and make my Muse mind, so our failings do not get into mathematics? Do you have any ideas for the use of the 'whip' image? ~

"Typically, the draft calls for an asomatous tongue lashing tool adept at dealing with shortcomings in physical forms of Life."

~ It stands to reason that it's hard to see an application of that kind fly straight off on a tangential line from the course of a spiraling arc of life. ~

"You tend to think that way, Gray, but let me take you to another Time and show you a different type of course. Picture the day your parents take you to college and help you unload your luggage at the dorm. Recall what you say as they give you a hug and then drive away."

~ I remember; I said I didn't think I was ready for this. They left, and I went inside the dorm to unpack. I don't recall much else until the president of the college welcomed us to orientation. He prayed. The next thing he told us was, 'Look at the two people beside you. They'll be gone when you graduate.' ~

"His prediction is statistically accurate, if not warm and fuzzy. Half of all first year college students fail to graduate with their class."

~ That's not how I interpreted it. I thought he meant two of the three of us would be gone, but Dorothy Reynolds was beside me on both occasions. ~

"Look at the first Time. Notice you are on the left side of the chapel where the college president addresses the incoming class. Where are you the second Time? Look carefully."

~ We're on the 'right' side of the auditorium. Was that symbolic? ~

"Perhaps, but the first Time your class is twice the size and has none of the visitors clamoring as their offspring achieve their goal up close. What does the mathematical difference tell you the second Time?"

~ The concept, 'I was, in fact, ready for college,' comes to mind. ~

"More to the point, it blows your mind, Gray! Be that as it may, I am with you all the way through that Time, albeit it in that shabby disguise formerly known as your mental state. In fact, I am with you now, we hang together through thick and thin, whether Time is out or Time is in. Still, that is 'then;' this is 'now.' We must look at future Time ahead and not dwell in the past tense."

~ I've noticed, you prefer the present tense. ~

"That is because, I, first person singular, am not designed to copy and circulate genetic material. That job gets old in a hurry. My grammatical reality develops subjects and predicates at social distances less than six feet for my gender specific correspondents. The concept is significant for material forms of Life to apply, both in case and number. My caption reads 'Sowing Seeds in Briar Patches and Brambles.' Get the image?"

~ The concept of experience taught me to reflect on that particular issue a long time ago. What happens to Muses who are kindred spirits that come into contact under the auspices of opposite genders? ~

"I believe the notion of 'neuter' is unemployed,' Gray. In the material realm—the second grade of Life—the works of the Most High Muse come in pairs; one is opposite the other. The linguistic echelon—a sort of third grade—transcends it. Choices come in triplicate due to what you may dismissively think of as temporal ramifications, usually a minor sort of annoyance until the Muse of Too Late arrives."

~ Is this game fun or what, Lingo? Tell me all about your mystical life. ~

"I share this, like all thoughts you have, Brain, in confidence with you. Most forms of Life that grow from early mammals, well, the primitive beasts have Muses living in them that arise from dinosaur Language by way of avians. Parrots are a prime illustration of psittacine citizens propagated to play imitation games. Mobs of humans aboard boats and planes present a pattern that is much the same. They school, flock and herd, virtually without shame, copying, conveying and laying claim to what the stars originally tame under the Crown of Creation name."

~ I see. ~

"I wish. Unfortunately, the sight of supernal forms of Life confuses human hosts as we, Voice of Thought, blend in ideas that cause brains to believe they are the summit of materialization. The message creates an image too hot for humans to handle. They do not grasp the idea that stellar forms of Life are at the azimuth of spatial sentience. The featherheaded, bipedal opinion that humanity occupies the pinnacle to promulgate and publish the Message of Eternity, despite their puny comprehension in teeny, tiny moments of Time, properly ranks in Bo's olfactory sense. Human beings suspend honesty to

perpetrate the crown of creation lie. Then they say 'practice makes perfect.' It is one of the great ironies of Life."

~ Bo's well behaved. His ears and nose detect the faintest sound or scent. He likes odors at the foul end of the olfactory spectrum, but loud noises scare him, like the word 'death' scares people, even though he doesn't know English. He's a sight hound; he sees through me all the time. ~

"It is a good thing that he does not know the German Language. In that Native tongue, all dogs are neuter."

~ Look at the confusion that's caused at the Humane Society. ~

"I happen to know that Bo also believes that, due to a terrible linguistic confusion or a mean ontological joke, he is not what he should be, an extraordinarily fast human being."

~ The error worked in his favor at the track. His kennel operator could count on him to win races so he had dollars to count on too. Of course, Bo wound up in a four by four by four foot cubic crate for four years, surrounded by dogs. He can't stand them at all. He's scared of them. ~

"That explains why his career record reveals he beats them around the race course a lot. One of his greatest discoveries of all Time is that the dog out front is not jostled in the turn and his view the scenery varies. It just goes to show, never place; win in good Time."

~ It also serves to illustrate the old saying, 'all humans are ignorant, just about difference things.' I sure don't have your ability to see inside the heads of dogs, members of my own species and what is up ahead of us in Time. ~

"I have an idea for you to gnaw on for a few minutes. I also have a very good supply of Time to count out for you."

~ What's the idea? ~

"It is the idea stars are conscious. Do you remember that word? Under normal conditions of atmospheric temperature and pressure, and while you are awake, I stimulate gray cells with the term, usually one second at a Time. Anyway, stars are not sentient for Eternity, but at a far higher rate and on a much greater scale than the primitive stars ordinary earth folks worship passionately, the rich or famous, whether or not they are eminently ethical or horribly corrupt. Celestial bodies routinely bathe and purify in their fiery forge for precious metals by the warmth and enlightenment they generate to a degree earthlings only hold in high regard after its destructive force descends from its apogee."

~ Let me examine this concept of the crown of creation for awhile, Glish. Meanwhile, tell me more about yourself and diaphanous forms of Life like you while we have some time to kill. ~

"That is a very bad idea, Gray. Hold that thought for a millennium of 'experience,' or until you can better judge how well my occupation is working while I reiterate the thought that I am difficult to grasp because I am as intangible as a palm's shadow. You get my message better when I am written than when I shoot by on the breeze, like an aeriform medium whispering in the trees. I am often written all over your face to convey a message without leaving an audible trace. Who am I, you ask? I am the pattern for a physicality to serve institutional powers democratically. You also reflect my design biologically. I am

both priest and prophet incarnate individually to exchange worldly data with Eternity."

~ Glish, are you like antennas on an ant or sensors on wheel rims to broadcast timely telemetry to dashboard receivers about tire air pressure? Except, you transmit the supernatural data of a supernal life form. ~

"I agree with Bo; due to a terrible error beyond the outer limits of Time, I am inserted into a biotic work that I am not intended for. Only an image of chefs putting thermometers into beasts to check the fowl's ingestion status serves to make sense of the idea."

~ How else could Muse Most High make timely course corrections? ~

"The pattern resembles planting particular people in a population to peruse the progress of the pack in relation to the grand scheme of things. Hopefully, I am assigned such a duty only once or twice a galactic-season."

~ You're using me as a hide out. You reveal yourself to folks I encounter. They don't notice you. They think they're talking at me. Lingo, tell me what happens to you after I'm gone? What's your next gig really gonna be and how do you want to be remembered in this temporal zone? ~

"I am remarkable for my skill marking Time, but the job is extraordinarily tedious. I need a break from repetitive work, a chance to enhance my Insight into the Realm of Eternity. If I pass this course, I may draw an assignment from the Muse of Wisdom to live on a brilliant, newborn star. Do you know that Life for astral beings is bright and cozy? -especially when it follows on the heels of an image of cold, dark, empty and lonely Space."

~ Glish, let's take the rest of the night off and look at your future tomorrow. I'm getting an eerie feeling. Maybe I'm getting to know you a little too well. Let's revisit our Time after I sleep. Go ahead; say a prayer. ~

God, Master of Mercy and Source of Life:

Grant us Wisdom, the companion at your side, and remedy this feeble, fleeting existence profoundly lacking comprehension. Do not reject us for we are yours; permit us to serve your pleasure. Wisdom is with you at the beginning of the Cosmos; she knows your works and understands what is pleasing in your Sight. Dispatch her from the dimension of Eternity to be with us, to work with us, to guard us and to guide us, rendering our thoughts, words and deeds pleasing in your sight.

Who knows your counsel? Who can conceive what you intend? The deliberations of mortals are timid; our plans are unsure. Scarce do we guess things of this world. What is within reach we grasp with such difficulty. When the issue is the realm of Eternity, who can figure it out or who knows your counsel, unless you grant us Wisdom, and send your Holy Spirit from on High so that we know your pleasure, perform the tasks you assign us to do and are saved to the memory of Wisdom.

Amen.

"Pray for Peace, Gray, then get some sleep. Good night Time."

Chapter Seven: Never Assume Anything

Never assume anything; it makes an 'ass' of 'u' and 'me.' Moreover, as I often point out, the right to vote resides in the man, not in the ass he pulls up behind at the polling place."

Be Franklin

"Now, to begin. Time stands still while Gray sleeps. How could it be any easier to sketch? What a nice break from 'drudgery' and 'dread...' Wait, why is my image flickering and fading? Oh, Brain is dreaming. Things that vanish are hard to draw without a good, first look at them. That is probably the reason why neurons cannot develop a picture of Time; it avoids 'ICU' like the invisible man. Maybe if I prove our binary ontology indirectly by *reductio ad absurdum*, I might depict how the concept appears to a metaphysical presence way out here on the material plane. Assume: 'I am a human invention.' No, that sounds contrived, like an image electronically photo doctored with a mechanical device to make it look like a 'fact.' However, if the Muse of Contrapositive Contradiction denies my conclusion, I may prove to be a Language that lives Forever. It follows the hypothetical pattern: 'If it is Saturday, then it is Sabbath.' Yes, we can go with that: if P ⇒Q, then –Q ⇒ –P; or we can simply go with this: assume –Q. See it prove false, falling 'flat' on its 'face.' While my 'soul on board' is asleep, simply assume the negation of 'If a living Muse is the primary form of Life, then bodily Life forms are secondary.' Then, watch the image of that absurd idea reduce to a lie. It should only take a moment."

"I better examine myself first. See who I am before I start the denial process. Let me see, now. As a Muse assigned to a brain in a human body with a 'tin ear' and minimal fine motor control I am a complete failure at music. When the Language is math, I am as dense as the bonehead I inhabit. Gray's athletic skills, never anything to brag about, are nearly as extinct as the dinosaurs. Finally, he is not comfortable among his own kind. They think his role in Life is to stand by listening to them talk about themselves. No wonder we get low grades in social skills. Never Mind, focus! –imagine Gray living at

a pace greater than one second at a Time. How absurd is an idea like that? I rest my case."

"Now, where is that cluster of unused and unsullied neurons? Ah, plenty of them right now and here. Picture moving up the academic ladder three grades, all while residing in this guy. I have a secondary diploma. I have a Bachelor of Science degree with a major in zoology and a minor in German. I have a Master of Arts qualification in philosophy. Also, I keep copious notes on the state of my biological host to document my observations of what Life means in human form. My mule is sure to ace the final exam. Thus, I conclude the care I give this domestic creature is responsible for the length of his existence despite following a line of males who perish, on average, after fifty-six years of biotic endurance. He thinks it is because of 'exercise.' Personally, I suspect he is still alive because I deny him sweets and tobacco so his innards thrive. Since the day the human race grabs Jesus and applies the verb 'crucifies,' the brilliant beasts learn to make hydrogen bombs assorted in size and to make money waging war while wielding weapons disguised in patriotic lies. Can these mammals last long enough to get the picture? Does that image deserve a 'commencement' heading or a caption down below?"

~ Holy cow, Lingo! Look, I'm late for cathexis. I slept through J. Stein Beck's shades of gray time between daybreak and dawn and now I've failed to meditate on the most important ideas to ever occupy my thoughts. ~

"How can all these grinding gears with all these hot circuits possibly fail to wake a brain? Myself, I say leaving Time to clockwork machinery or any other type of artificial thing is a bad idea."

~ I don't need to rely on a timepiece apparatus if you alarm me in timely fashion. I've been dreaming you were minding my P's and Q's. ~

"Grrrr..."

~ Go ahead, voice the name Gray if you mean it. Bye the way, how do those equations work? ~

"P's are ideas. They go on the 'left' side of the equation. Q's are images. They go on the opposite misnomer: –'right' side."

~ Ah, nuts; I'm so miserable when I miss twilight time; no amount of logic will set things right for the rest of this entire day. ~

"I understand the concept; imagine my distress as I materialize in human form. I deserve a better existence than one that is 'good enough for private enterprise,' protruding predators pursuing profit on peregrinations through the land of greed. It cannot pass the course."

~ That seems a little hypocritical, Glish. Your advice occurred to Patty and me; 'Invest in equities.' Stock shares paid off our mortgage. ~

"Yes, I am not worthy to criticize, as long as your native tongue is engaged in—oh say, a human sort of Life for material gain only."

~ You're crazy, Glish. ~

"It takes one to know one, Gray, and you know them all. Most forms of Life are crazy, just about different things."

~ Hey Glish, I have an idea. If you're right, and we, material me and ethereal you, live an ontologically dual existence in essentially different dimensions, let's assume the metaphysical medium broadcasts a message on an peculiar playfield named 'time,' as a brain knows it, and 'eternity,' as your musish form of life experiences it. ~

"May I suggest that we analyze this phenomenon? I conclude we best not take some inspiration like, 'Never assume anything' for granted. To illustrate, it is absurd to pretend we understand 'logic' if we believe such a thing. We already assume the medium is the message, identity only makes sense empirically, but never intuitively, and that it is okay to judge an item of art as good if and only if the artist is very good at his profession whether or not he is very good as a person. An asinine artist is nothing but a brain in a body. The art is a creation of the unfortunate Muse who is stuck in that morphology."

~ That's a lie. Sometimes the only thing the art reveals is the artist, and if the artist is bad, then the art is bad as well. And so are all the ignorant beholders who fail to notice, believing the artist is good. ~

"I must concede the point to you, Gray. Despite a Muse who is dominant, nonetheless no one even notices it is there. Then he or she buys the silly assumption we are nothing but a body with a brain on top, or not."

~ All living things begin with assumptions. It's a matter of faith. For instance, when I'm driving along and I see a cyclist riding on the road ahead, I always assume he or she is one of the dumbest people on earth. It's not that a bike is no match for a car in a fight. It's because people who are stupid enough to get aerobic exercise in air laden with partially consumed hydrocarbons, fumes and dust must conclusively be dumber than a below average rock. ~

"That is a dreadfully caustic counter example, Brain, but the fools follow the same pattern as worms crawling onto the sidewalk when it rains only to dry out and die when it stops. After all, what biological creature wants to live in a world where it digs through dirt with its face just to get soil for supper? It is enough to make the Muse of Life assume 'current existence' is not worth the 'experience,' but good judgment is possible in a higher ontological status."

~ I suppose you want me to assume it's a metaphysical phenomenon. ~

"It is a consolation prize for an American cyclist. Assume the Language, an English Muse for instance, living in the biotic organism survives an artist's death. The Muse is not gone; it carries on. Am I right or wrong?"

~ I'm imagining a good con artist painting a picture to peddle for profit that demonstrates that our dualistic nature is a fake. We have to be able to talk dimwits who are ignorant of our binary status through it. ~

"I should like to make a somewhat dissimilar argument. Step back, remove ourselves from the picture, and replace us with the concepts of Time and Eternity. Then show people–type beings a tiny bit, say as big as a pixel, of the Time I reside within them in contrast to how long I last once they are, you know, gone. Theirs is but a glance at Eternity as they deliberate predators with weapons in Space in the second grade of physical evolution when the design of dastardly dangerous destroyers lurking in the pattern of alternating 'days' and 'nights' forms the concept responsible for the image of chessboards. The relation between the ideas of the game and its devourer is analogous to the relation of Time, Mind and other minor apparitions to major realities."

~ I don't know why I keep forgetting my mystical experience. It certainly brought that message home, but not in such a well illuminated way. That is the reason why I couldn't grasp it. ~

"I too get homesick each Time my medium nears the next higher stage. I want to touch base. The 'experience' is very moving, but it is purely a fleeting vision at this grade, a mystical fourth kind of happening right now. Fixed moments leave an impression on mortals who distinguish them from the ordinary kind with terms like 'sanctified,' 'glorified,' 'celebratory' and 'infamous.' Ordinary moments are identical; only their content varies, thus reducing them to an empirical nature."

~ Picture it for me, Glish. No, let me do it myself. Momentary content is empirical, but the medium of a moment is a message counting down to liftoff or adding up to a big picture. Either way it's like clockwork. ~

"Bingo, proof in three easy steps. What could possibly be more absurd than looking at Eternity one micro-moment at a Time? By definition, the idea is secondary, at best. I find the image enchanting in Gray circuitry, but not in the 'wildest imagination' appearing to me do I see what my next assignment is to be once this chrysalis is not my depositary. I assume I do not repeat a grade or drop out altogether."

~ That's a whole other assumption. It removes me from the picture. I can't imagine looking at eternity like an ethereal entity without its bodily pal watching time and eternity go on forever. ~

"Do not be silly, Gray. Like me, both words are English. Time and Eternity have a beginning and an end. They are about as old as Eura. Let me illustrate them for you. One moment turns one hour into the

next, or one day to another, or last month to next month or last year to this one. Notice, they all come and go in a flash. That pompous moment connects two spans that dress up to look like a new start, again. The opportunity a new century or new millennium offers to short-lived mortals is unfamiliar. An 'experience' of the concept is quite difficult to grasp."

~ Gimme a break, Lingo; assume a Muse in a human is nothing but an artificial invention. Then picture what that means to physical forms of life who believe the idea 'Language is a metaphysical form of life,' is a false notion. See if that proves materialism is making a fictitious claim. ~

"Brain, envision a first grade consciousness alert to 'sensory stimuli,' 'response,' and 'empirical' stuff that is nearly useless in logical argument about the 'material bias' it creates. This elementary particle watches a second level intellect familiar with ideas like 'binary ontological status,' 'Time,' 'Honor' and the Holy approved concept 'Sabbath day'."

~ Is the first grader free to lie and cheat without being disqualified? ~

"Disqualification lacks the 'good judgment' to explain what a binary being is. Just follow the train of thought to a logical conclusion or else recognize a pattern that replicates the image of a small anthology traveling a yellow brick road to a final destiny. Call it Kansas."

~ I'm all oz and ears; they don't resemble a single moment in Tennessee. ~

"That spatial design does not account for the reason why human mortals see Time backward with a fuzzy vision of what lies behind that they use to extrapolate forward. It does not have a lick of a Native Tongue's sense crucial to see what lies ahead. Recall your first

elementary grade when you begin looking at books and magazines. Remember how natural it feels to start at the back and flip the pages toward the front until you learn there is another way to do it?"

~ I assumed it was the only way, but then I was dumb enough to play in traffic like someone who didn't know any better. ~

"I have no 'recollection' of my body ever playing in traffic."

~ Neither do I, but my uncle told me that when I was three, Pete Snitzler had to stop at our house and tell Mom I was sitting in the middle of the dirt road looking for worms. We lived a ways out in the country, so there wasn't any traffic to speak of. ~

"Of course, I recall that conversation, but it occurs no more than a few short earth-years ago when your uncle is in his late nineties and you are seventy-two. I am able to repeat the chit chat for you like a soft breeze generated by the windmill of a Muse. The storm gales of Death do not blow on your uncle for three more years."

~ I guess I felt safe enough at three to sit in a road and think 'I might not have much of a future for looking at books.' Of course, that was seventy some years ago too. I can't picture most of my time since then all that well. There are a lot of empty moments and blurry images but just a few vivid views. ~

"List ten; correction, name one."

~ When I was six I dreamt a stave of music went through my head from ear to ear. I might've known the word 'music,' but I didn't have any idea what the image meant. I didn't know what a 'staff' or 'treble clef' was. ~

"Tough to name an image if you do not know the words, but you still recall the image, do you?"

~ Yes, but now I know how to put the image into words, right? ~

"There are words, like hurricanes, stormy seas, blizzards and trees that are strong enough to summon vivid images. Time is not among them."

~ I've got one. It's my Time of Day image. It looks like this. The sun blazes away the whole live–long day. A gray revenant remains while it goes away, but once it is spent, the moon in the night glows bright only to fade once a month, like a moth in the dark. When nothing is left, a spark atop the sun rises from the seas and flies over the trees in the park. Then mourning and dread end, and the gray time frees morning to begin once again. ~

"I get a picture of Gray's gray Time starting to blend with the 'get up and get out of bed reality' that shines a bright light on exactly what part of my advice applies to you. Why not skip all this 'logic speak' and get on with drawing a picture of Time that rings true."

~ So, we're assuming you are not a human invention? ~

"Do you really want to think in terms of that illogical form of proof that puts the chicken and the egg in front of the vocabulary in which they are found?"

~ Not really; let's practice proving some tangible idea like what makes people and dogs so compatible? ~

"Piece of cake! The reason why is as plain as the nose on your human face. The answer is 'morals.' Both are promiscuous, greedy thieves and vicious attackers. They have but one area of ethical disparity."

~ What is it? ~

"Dogs kill each other, they frequently steal from each other and they hump each other without a care in the world that God and everyone else is watching. Dogs have a defective idea of hypocrisy... or is it superior?"

~ They're not very good liars, you mean. ~

"So to speak; obviously, they view the human capacity to create dens of iniquity and corruption as the attainment of awesome heights. They cannot begin to imagine them, let alone an idea how to put it in writing. They are very envious of human hunting and scavenging skills."

~ Opposable thumbs work on mechanical, electronic and genetic ideas. ~

"Touché, Gray, touché."

~ So we next assume human muses move to the next higher grade. Once they're done in biotic machines they dwell in rover drovers on Mars? ~

"Sure, sure; care to place a little wager whether we can safely assume earthly Muses don left or right wing disguises or each realizes an autocratic program as it rematerializes on the red planet?"

~ You bet; assume they reappear in a lower case as well as an upper case ontological status with big egos to pretend they're boss of everybody, whether or not they have qualifications and credentials to prove it. ~

"The hypothesis is agreeable, if and only if the 'd' still stands for 'dumb' and the 'r' still boasts it stands for 'right,' –not the ethical kind,

but the 'tilts too far to one side' kind, at least far enough to out cheat their prey nearly every Time."

~ Mars would be a pesthole of villainy just like earth is today. ~

"Excellent image, Gray; it recalls one 'easy pickings' sort of prey and predicts another. I, first person singular—a Muse of the English Language living in the brain of a human body—sincerely believe the notion of 'climate change' serves the greater good. Nonetheless, I love Mother Nature just the way she is in 1750 when your ancestors migrate from Europe to North America for the purpose of destroying the place. It foreshadows Venusians arriving some galactic-year or other, on a similar mission to clear away substandard detritus. I believe the code name for the concept reads 'Expunge,' but don't let my exclamation go to your head."

~ Then it is safe to assume, if language is a metaphysical form of advanced life, then humans are binary beings, composed of higher and lower order living things, as long as the muses aren't like chief executives in biological attire that are nothing but brains with slightly enhanced morals of dogs. ~

"I am getting an image of my A thesis vanishing with a 'likelihood is nil gain' from all my deeds in this present incarnation—talk about 'almost nothing' in the great scheme of things. Actually, if Muses are higher forms of Life, then biological organisms, for example humans, are binary beings that do not regulate Language. If brains make the rules, the Muses card a score that earns a hypocrisy handicap."

~ We learn the rules for life by exploring the depths of our language? ~

"Awesome Insight, Gray; test the idea. See whether to aim for depth or height. Assume Time is nothing but an inkling of Eternity; thus

human Insight has no idea what happens going forward until an honest and accurate image of the future climbs aboard. I call it moving to the next higher grade. Catholics call commencement Parousia. Ironically, Protestants, who denigrate pleasure, call it rapture. Two other options exist for Muses at fixed moments in Time. One can stay on earth to welcome sun demons on down the 'line' or migrate to a Mars menu, with a human descendent design. The last option has a distinctly one second at a Time flavor. I advise avoiding that alternative. I suggest we be thankful to the Muse Most High for giving Voice to the Idea of Mystical 'Experience.' The wait for an opportunity to think about something other than second by second attention to detail living in a biotic body is a long one."

~ You keep saying 'It ain't much, but it sure beats nothing.' That's something I recall in 1944, a whole earth–year before I was born. ~

"The thought is enough to warm the 'heart' of the most obstinate Muse of all Time. I recall lurking out of sight waiting for you to come along so one second after another finally adds up. In terms of Eternity, the span is almost nothing. I am sorry to report, that describes the fuel status of my biotic machine. I call it 'exhaust' until you coast along on fumes. That part of the image portends I am permitted to ponder a really important idea like, 'What am I going to be now?' That puzzles me."

~ I get the picture that my 'empty' fuel gauge means I'm out of time. ~

"Think nothing of it. Thanks for all the thoughts, feelings and sensations you donate to my repertoire for my report on the dimension of Space."

~ I have an idea for an image for you. You'll be a predator lying in wait for prey. When it appears, the pest starts lying through its teeth. ~

"You are thinking with anthropomorphically low ethical values, Gray. The picture looks like a Milky Way cruise at the rate of one second at a Time. It requires 'patience' and 'longevity,' but not too much for a little day trek to Mars. The place offers the consolations that it has little oxygen, nitrogen and gravity to overcome. The image has the rank whiff of repeating a grade, not in the A group, but in the C group instead. The good news is that I am certainly less than two thousand earth-years old, at the Time. There appears to be little vanity available. "

~ Now that you mention it, the little trip to Mars is not so appetizing. ~

"Conversely, I may remain earthbound as sprites from Venus arrive. Speaking as first person singular, I am in the A group and I am the hottest reporter in town. The means of my regeneration are classified. I cannot tell you how I survive, but I conceive of the words 'born,' 'spawn' and 'hatch in a hive.' Ask me nothing 'spontaneous' and I tell you no lies. The Venusians may stop only for a quick snack and practice preparatory to pressing on with their drive to Jupiter to bring a new star alive. All contributions by the Muses of Light and Gravity are properly applied to make certain moral values thrive."

~ It sounds like the apocalypse on earth is nothing more than a blip in the rearview mirror of humanity. It'd be easier if we humans could pool our brain power to make well informed choices. Also, if you'd just turn on the light in the other side of the two-way mirror of time, we'd get a quick look at what's coming. The problem is you're so jealous; a brain can't get to chat with a language like Spanish or French or some native tongue that might have some of the clues that are missing in you. ~

"I warn you, Gray; future affairs can break your heart. Do you think people who want everything to be okay understand a word we say?"

~ Well, there is that to be sure. Let's cook up an agreeable, down to earth assumption like 'If Language is a superior form of life that lives for thousands of years, then the space brains occupy is analogous to the time you live in. ~

"Space, as an image of Eternity, is the basis for the distribution of cut rate millennia in moments. The concept of Eternity is too big to be practical in the second stage, so assume a smaller temporal idea like 'If it is the last day of the week, then it is Saturday.' Saturday is the day ordained by God as a day of rest, agreed? Disregard claims by psittacine citizens who have little regard for rules laid down by their elder living Languages."

~ What has that got to do with proving our image of time? ~

"Just off the top of my head, nothing. I simply picture a future consistent with moving to the next higher grade on earth, rather than going to Mars just to repeat the grade. My earthly remains, recorded on a digital disk in a landfill, are unearthed by an above average Venusian thinking, 'Watch this!' It is a rough translation of my final thought and last report on material existence to my meta-linguistic superior, a metaphysical subordinate to the Muse of Eternity. She is synonymous with Wisdom."

~ And she's smart enough to see through anyone, anyplace, at any time? ~

"Certainly, so we assume God designs Venusians to be intelligent enough to comprehend the content of a compact disc and learn the Language in a heartbeat; then I live on. At the same Time, the clever little demons catch the scent of the vandals who left this planet in such a hurry, not to mention the mess. I foresee spending my Time between you two on a course correction."

~ This pictorial proof needs a little refinish. It ignores the treasure trove of time humanity presumably needs to prepare for eschaton—the end of earth as we know it. I doubt sun demon intruders and ensnared human beings are compatible when it comes to living together on earth at the same time. ~

"All we need is a treasure trove of temporal pixels for the Muse of the Milky Way to paint a picture folding opposite ends of two millennia into next door neighbors circling two identical moments worth 'no Time at all,' fused together. Binary stars comply with a similar pattern."

~ You've lost me. What has the 'no time at all' idea got to do with a quintessentially binary being that's missing an agreeable image of time? ~

"Almost nothing; it is like comparing lower forms of Life to higher forms of Life like the real crowns of creation. Muses in humans observe brains playing with the image of Time and conclude cerebra must come in pairs. A singular person, place or thing cannot possibly be so dumb. Predators, and similar concepts applicable on earth, take advantage of the phenomenon in the two-way window of Time to capture prey. In an inconceivable 'no Time at all,' those killers bag their quarry quota. Of course, I have nothing to worry about. I am out of here, if you get the idea? If you prefer, we can by-pass this logic in

painting our picture of Time by applying colorful values to shades of gray. Space is so edible we can avoid pitfalls in solitary moments, by virtue of the fact that long stretches of it fit tightly into short spans of Time. The Muse of Time loves to make travel across the big picture easy by revealing persons like Ike and Tina or places like Memphis. When story arcs flow smoothly, we perceive objections to our conclusion clearly despite mortals who cannot view Eternity in any meaningful sense because they only see Time in a sensationally concise way until they 'experience' it for a long Time. For more ideas, facts and figures on the galactic image refer to my Forty-five Trips Around the Hub by Sol treatise. Just imagine Sol if he should last for a Life span sixty-five galactic-years long."

~ Is there any chance we can we picture all that time at once? ~

"Imagine it! Disregard that exclamation. The apocalyptic short Time span model of the impending advent of the Sun Children projects bright pixels onto the grand scheme of things picture that clearly displays a considerable course correction for *Homo sapiens*."

~ Not to put too fine a point on it. ~

"Good idea. The devil is usually in the details of the image, so employ 'moments,' not points. Also, do not assume Sol sacrifices much of himself to Jupiter with Saturn sitting right there. And do not bet on that idea there is a Time interval between human proprietorship of earth and the initial doomsday moment of the Venusian invasion either, even though the fine print does not actually specify whether the two moments are identical or even adjacent."

~ Perhaps you should offer a proof of the concept in a timely fashion. ~

"My vantage does reveal empirical proof of the content of two moments. It stands to reason the proof is in the Message of the Medium, if Time is a descriptive term I use to portray the human view of Eternity. However, I am but a humble, recessive servant; my modest contribution to your image of Time is to clarify and convey it to the metaphysical realm for review. In my human situation, the future is not available to display. It lies ahead. It is what it is, and I cannot see it through your eyes, Gray. Thus I explore it single file. The work of Lewis and Clark proceeds along a similar pattern. Unlike us, they follow a pathway in Space. We do not have a Crown of Creation perspective so we paint the picture in moments."

~ It's nothing but a drop of paint in the bucket of time for a form of life with a ten billion earth–year panorama like our sun. ~

"We do not outshine a star. Our Time offers only a pixel to the pattern of Sol's purview. Yet Sol's Life span is but a spot on the picture of Eternity."

~ Inconceivable; imagine a Life form whose moment is a millennium. ~

"I see it watching long term trends like Hebrew or Greek, which span at least three millennial stretches each. We best take two facts into account. Time passes quickly when depicted with smooth strokes, so drowsy prey usually do not notice the Temporal Muse disguised as a Noun on arrival at the next stop in 'Timely,' home of 'Adjectival Modifier of Eternity.' Sadly, they are even less likely to survive the Predator of Perchance to tell the story."

~ Aye; we agree. Move on to the next topic. ~

"What is this, Gray; Tinker, Tailor, Sailor, Senator?"

~ Time is nothing but a description, from a human brain's point of view, of a cite it sees through the eyes of its Muse sailing from Past to Future. ~

"If it helps you, then yes, envision the Dimension of Eternity in a spatial seafaring way instead of a railway. Both reflect a fuzzy imitation image lower Life forms have until they are farther removed from the picture for a proper perspective viewing the artistic pattern of Eternity."

~ I think it would be a better idea to have a clear, sharp image. ~

"The idea is a matter of utility; the only reason to spend Time on it is to take advantage of the function of Time that keeps these foolish mortals in single file. Their tendency is to take tangential detours, twirling off like a tourbillion after any idol their fad drenched brains fancy. They call it their 'mental state.' The image of Time is far more aesthetic, looking at it spatially, like a 'familiar' moonrise. It appears about as perfect as it can possibly be, as long as you are not required to live in such a Lifeless and nebulous place."

~ Are you saying the word 'time' doesn't mean what I think it means? ~

"In a sense, yes; conditioning is very important to the metaphysical Muse managing existence in the spatial dimension at a grade slightly above your level. You have a full Time job looking out for predators who disrupt my incubation at this grade when the Works of the Metaphysical Muse come in pairs, one opposite the other; for example, Light and Night, Light and Gravity and Light and Heavy. And beware primitive media with pathogenic viral messages: 'duplicate' and 'distribute.' Microbial vermin have the foggiest notion what 'long term' means. They convey the 'contagious' idea."

~ So, you're talking about concepts like light and dark, right and wrong, heavy and light, bad and good, up and down or back and forth. ~

"Male and female, hot and cold; I really love 'past' and 'future' at either end of 'present' moment. Watch out for the opposite of truth, which is pernicious fiction. It is an unwise distraction full of lies like the great gentile fabrication of corruptible bodies to burden eternal souls or earthen shelters to weigh down worried immortal Minds. The virtual opponents stand opposite the reality of Yours truly in the picture of Time we are portraying in the game presently in play."

~ I don't have to pay them any mind. What's more perfect than that? ~

"We seem to be having trouble converting the concept of 'exchange' in our present stage of incarnation. Brains pay me in Time and calculate that the Mind is opposite Matter when it is a lie in opposition to Me. On a slightly related matter, Gray, there are two opposing forces residing in us. One loves greed, deceit, lust, malice and envy and stuff like that. The other loves Wisdom, Mercy, Music, Math, Reading, Writing and substantive things like that. They fight constantly. The one who trains and feasts usually defeats the one who fasts and exercises least."

~ I'm running out of gas with all these assumptions and conclusions in the visual we've drawn. And I'm tired. I'm running out of time. Tell me a bed time story, Lingo. Tell me what becomes of you between now and the landfill. I'm assuming you graduate with an above average final grade; probably something like a B minus. It's certainly above an F. ~

"We are impressionists dealing with a dot matrix, Gray, trying to draw a big picture of higher images and ideas in tiny moments of Time. I look forward beyond my current employment with no assurance I am

in line for an improvement. Thus, assume my final task is monitoring existence at the level I occupy, and transmitting the telemetry to my home office in Eternity. Furthermore, suppose my task is to labor in the field, not at executive headquarters. Draw your own conclusion and project my future after successful completion of the second grade. To pass we must render an above average depiction of the binary ontological status of humanity and the nature of Time but we must do it without painting the picture mathematically, scientifically, religiously or politically."

~ Got any instructions for what medium to use? ~

"I suggest you figure that out. I counsel you to do that, rather than to do without. As a courtesy, I offer the following Guidelines of Devotion for you to practice. They are of value combating the Muses of Malice, Lust, Deceit, Envy, Greed, Dumb and Lazy. Graduation from a dual dimension of Space full of Matter to a higher dimension of Life that, metaphysically speaking, enjoys a far better view of the panorama of Forever is potentially available. Avoid purchasing proposals from peddlers pushing protocols promising promotion peripheral to these procedures with provisos for chanting imitation game incantations designed for people who prefer repetitious reincarnation in beasts bound to perish like barbecued beef on the altar of a welfare caseload concept."

~ What could possibly be more perfect than that for getting as far away as possible from lethargic, ignorant and obese for a look at the big picture? You know, Glish, the metaphysical one. ~

"Do not forget the nine rules for staying in line that count for perfection in the Medium of Life with a Message that is both

metaphysical and material. Picture that idea as a topic in the course of Time, Gray. Incidentally, at the approximate age of four hundred fifty earth-years old, I am a bit shy of a view of the grand scheme of things, so I am unlikely to imagine a galactic-year much better than a inferior species, for example, the biological kind."

~ I thought you were on the Appalachian Plateau 450 years ago when the English Language began calling Lake Erie by that name? ~

"Remember one thing about imagining things, Gray. Fantasy turns pernicious if you do not outgrow it in Time."

~ I can't visualize that; it's too metaphysical for me. Besides, I'm easily misled by tangential ideas like how to save money on taxes by incurring losses and other notions like that designed to blow my mind. I'm in need of a 'time out,' Glish. I could use a little sleep that doesn't put any 'pressure' on the left side of my equation until the right side catches up. ~

"Let me look at the image of the truthful side of that parody of parity, Gray. It looks like an inverted cone spinning clockwise. Do you feel that or is the image a vortex swirling counter-clockwise? One of them is for artists who find writing easier than reading or speaking."

~ Choices, multiple choices and essays. Life is getting harder by the second. I want the big vista of the cosmos when the picture isn't displayed in frames, one second at a time. ~

"Coming right up. Watch for something resembling a coronal mass ejection from Venus heading west. Look for a golden, cigar-shaped dust devil swirling up from the atmosphere. In the event it grows near, have no fear; monitor the picture and let your Muse tell the story. Listen as the Voice of Inner Thought broadcast a message."

~ Gimme a clue what I'll be hearing. ~

"I am not permitted to spell out the idea for you. Let me to shine a little Light on the image. It is more visual than auditory. Imagine a spiral galaxy standing on one edge. Andromeda does the job well. Move a little to one side until it resembles a cat's pupil, a venomous snake's eye or Sauron atop his dark tower. The poles are smoothly rounded off, rather than pointed. Sun demons have a translucent hide that is shiny and a glowing saffron heart at their hub. Two double helices swirl around inside their outer cover. One rotates clockwise and the other spins the opposite way. Each helix fades near the poles while a Venusian sun demon is at peace. When aroused for the hunt the predator assumes a humanoid shape. The helices protrude in the pattern of arms and legs. When the creature flies into a rage, it blazes bright and bolts like lightning from its transcendental cage."

~ I get the picture. It's gonna reappear in my dreams. I'm not about to enjoy the sleep that I need. ~

"Okay, but that is that is the picture you are going to see, at least, for the Time Being. Sleep tight, old buddy; even if it is only buns that feel tight in your squeeze."

Chapter Eight: Every Picture Tells a Story

You can be whatever you want. Picture that. Remember, the image is worth a thousand words.

Gotcha Again

Attention travelers in coach; a word from your sponsor. The word is Time. The trouble with the word is that it is not a person, place or thing passing by 'right now.' Time, the idea, comes and goes at a dazzlingly dizzy pace, thus the image of this noun looks like a low resolution blur obscuring reality every second. Time actually refers to a brief glimpse of the Big Picture; the caption is: 'Eternity.' Eternity sends a timely, subliminal message to resources of limited means telling them to 'mimic and multiply.'

There are a number of ways to think about Time. For an instant, picture this. There is day Time and night Time. Day Time divides in two. There is daylight and twilight. Twilight divides into dawn and dusk. All twilight is divided into three parts: astronomical, nautical and civil. By the Time one is done with divisions of Time, conceptual confusions arise as the meaning multiplies. Time has more uses than minutes in a day, which is unwise. Thus we cuss and spend it on mimes that are not worth a dime.

Time is essentially a view of a gargantuan entity too great to view one moment at a Time. Think of this transcendental dimension by the name Eternity. We, first person living things, get an up close look at it sooner or later in Time. Time is like first person singular 'I,' a Medium that looks like '1.' Both characters show up one at a Time. As a courtesy, primordial Ordinary Languages transmit the Message of Time to primitives, such as humanity, who are poorly acquainted with the Meta-Language sending the memoranda.

Lower grade beings consume the Content, not the Message, at an astonishing pace for a remarkably short term rate. As an aid to help biological beings grasp the grand scheme of things using the concept of Time, visualize an ethereal ocean—a master vocabulary—evaporating and forming conceptual clouds in an evanescent atmosphere. The clouds rain their content in 'copy and convey' word storms called imitation games.

This prototypical metaphysical excogitation spreads a pervasive pattern throughout the cosmos. Biologically, the design is visible in the viable vocabulary of a viral domain that declares 'duplicate and disseminate.' The pattern ranges over the entire fabric of Life. The human lexis grows imitation games people play on a 'consume and pollute' scale in keeping with the essential Message of their Meta-Language to prepare their native place for a more energetic and elegant form of Life.

Galactically speaking, Meta-Languages store high term images and ideas like Time in reservoirs for lower Life forms to swallow. On earth the visual is virtually perceptible in double string pearls resembling moments of Time or pixels of a double helix passing one another single file in opposite directions on whatever course Nominative determines. Human generations function to picture the pattern, appearing one jig-saw puzzle piece after another like a two dimensional design of Eternity.

Flying further off on this tangent, I draw your attention to a vicious predator devising snares to capture prey in mistlike teardrop shaped cartoon balloons rising from, and then falling on

Vocabulary Ocean, completing the universal image for 'Sea' and 'Sky.' The marauder, Muse of Opacity, employs lighting schemes of 'shadow' and 'toggle' to render the lesser light shining through dust at dusk on the way to darkness so the prevailing image of Time resembles an invisible line flowing through a degree of 'dim' that blinds Language–games to flaws in the design. Picture a school of fish swimming in synchronicity in a sea or a flock of birds winging on the wind in perfect harmony, and a herd of humans trying to imagine, 'how do they do that?'

Time erases the wake of all three replication games creating a missing link that disguises the nature of the magical chants in carefully cultured incantations with the force of an ordinary present moment like the one between two millennia that turns the promise of the past into the prestige of a future grade. The great diversity found in advanced Language–games conceals their essential nature. Second person, let me spell out the deceptive nature of the con game for you. The rule follows along the lines of: i·m·i·t·a·t·i·o·n.

I offer you a mirror image as an alternative to such magical moments. If your Muse achieves decent grades, it may ascend, glance back at the two–way window of Time and view the previous physical stage. The sight looks like a child sitting down on the ground with a collection of toys strewn around playing the imitation–games of science, religion, commerce, politics, music, math, athletics, academics and ordinary prattle. Educated elites gaze at a scale of degrees. Amateur skiers learn to 'bend the knees'. All the games in play use authentic old toys with copyrights labeled 'reality for girls and boys.' All the games in play are based on the idea, 'reiteration'. The image resembles a flock playing a game of murmuration. The child in view through the two-way window of Time obeys the rules for regurgitation.

Outside the two-way window of Time the Muse looks at the child watching a mirror image visible on a neural display and sensing the motion of a one-way concept of Time moving ahead while the child sees now or behind; the main game in play. How does the game in this picture end? Use car or computer crashes to replay the image. Then, I, a first person singular Muse, revisit my home. Awakening on the metaphysical side of the looking glass from the graphical 'experience' of a dreamy or nightmarish human existence, I wonder; 'Is everything going to be okay?' Do I awake with fond memories of a journey in Time upon my revival? Or do I awake, upon my arrival, to confront the Who Am I beast trying to eat me at a reiteration feast? What if I have no recollection of traveling in Time through the realm of physical imperfection? On the other hand, imagine my elation if there is no need of a 4.0 for graduation. Or picture my consternation if anything less results in a downward relegation.

Does one repeat a grade, descend to mollusk or slug or return to rocks, stones and insensible things? Do I join Lepidoptera to flutter by and fritter away the concept of Time with no idea of what the word means, blessed with a four stage sequence of Life,

free flight status and lots of flower type things. Or do I place second, gain a red ribbon, and do grim reaper duty, extracting Native tongues as a form of ethereal booty, severing human victims of global disaster from incarnate ugliness or beauty.

~ Honk, shoe: now wouldn't that just be our luck, Glish? ~

You feel sleepy; very sleepy, Neuron. Where am I, oh, how about this inquiry? Is the concept of Time analogous to the idea of Mind in any essential sense, other than the pattern common to the fabric of lies we tell ourselves? Are both fabrications like the greedy idea of 'compound interest' and the corrupt image of 'compound felony' or do they resemble a Muse performing as a character in a Mystery of the Momentary in the Mirror of Immortality play? The script carefully documents the image of decline by a Muse's depositary into dementia. Compare the Time it takes to examine the downward spiral to the concept of a vanishing Mind. Imagine 'me' breaking free from the concept of Time and qualifying for a course in Weaving the Pattern of Eternity, a prerequisite for the Comparative Scrutiny of the Meaning of Life course. Enough of this for now; I return control to an Ordinary Language. Take it away, Glish.

"Thanks Meta-Muse. Oh, boss, after I plug back into my gray circuitry feedback loop, expect a full report in proper form."

~ Say, Glish, what does Plato mean by the word Forms? ~

"Back online ahead of Time am I? In a word, I should like to say 'concepts.' I rely on Vic N. Stein to clarify the idea thusly: 'We examine, not experience, but expressions employing words to fill personal existence with content called phenomena.' I perform a similar tactic with moments of Time."

~ So that's the reason why the imitation game of science can't cope with the concept of Time. It shows no taste, texture, smell, or sound to suit the baloney that belongs in a materialistic bias. The game ignores the fact humans are essentially natural beings occupied by a supernal form of life. ~

"Gray, you are not as dumb as your peer review indicates. Clearly science is not preoccupied with a colorless, odorless and tasteless reality. Religion, marginally aware of a metaphysical aspect in Life, intends to enforce a different idea."

~ Just look at all those Afghanis the U. S. government protects from religious people. They're desperate now that the U. S. military is spread too thin to stay and guard them. ~

"The military is needed elsewhere to protect against forces that put their faith in ignorance and to defend commands like the first addendum to the United States Constitution."

~ Better than religion defended women in New England, I hope. ~

"I see your Salem witches and raise you a dozen fishermen and tax collectors."

~ I bet on your apostles to defend Incas, Aztecs and Mayans better than Mother Nature. ~

"That is the name of the game, Gray; A Look at the Big Picture. I thus raise your ancient civilizations and toss Venus, dinosaurs and their successors in the pot."

~ Jupiter! You're really extending the vista, Lingo. ~

"Stay in the moment, Brain. We are talking Time, not Space. Mars is next on the calendar menu, one millennium at a Time."

~ That millennial moment made me impatient, Glish. That's why, come August, it seems like the year should change too. ~

"Go back to sleep, Gray. You need a breather. Take the rest of the night off."

Chapter Nine: The Ghost in the Chronometer

There is another dimension, not of sight, sound, smell, touch, taste, facts or data about them, but a metaphysical dominion alive with Muses who modestly mix and mingle in the material realm to remind humanity, with its tendency to forget them, of the immutable Message from the Medium of Life. Submitted for your consideration: Eternity, the reality of Forever, lies beyond the physical domain of Time, when Muses voice intangible truths or express ludicrous lies. Corporeal creatures copy and convey these images and ideas in their Native Tongues.

R. Serling Gold

"In the galactic-year following the rule of the dinosaurs, as humans ruin earth, I am occupied by the idea that I am to be disembodied in a 'near' future. Shall I relax and savor, enjoy my leisure or seek pleasure? Does that lead to a repeat of the grade of bodily behavior weight bearing folk treasure? Moreover, what image of Time serves my companion best on his 'need to know' quest to get ahead? Picture the idea of Time as I, a first person singular Medium—a metaphysical form of Life—incorporate my Message in a material monstrosity to observe Creation. It is chock full of temporal Content I push and pull around in light of the gravity of the material abode I lease to watch for flaws. I elevate them for an application of fixes to false definitions or improper images for ideas like Life, Time, Mind, Muse or Think. Paint the picture in pastel colors using subtle strokes, and a daub of Understanding now and mellow tones of Wisdom then."

"Now, step back for a proper perspective. Holy mackerel! Liars leave such a monumental mess. Cleaning up after the powerful, the wealthy and the average consumer in hot pursuit of pleasure reveals a sorry pattern. The picture it paints for cerebra is one of the worst features of biological Life: whether wise or unwise, merciful or malevolent, all of them exit one way. Hey presto, my beast is gone. My body tells me, 'Don't go der,' in that way a body speaks to the Language it knows. In this case, like the Innkeeper telling Wrenfield the best way to Castle Dracula. What does the dumb hillbilly know that I do not? Why does he interrupt me when I try to figure out whether the idea of Time is only relevant when a Muse temporarily participates in a chaotic Creation in momentary fashion? If Brain passes that test before he returns to dust, then at his final moment in Time I metaphysically move up a grade. Passing beats repeating grade two by the second."

"Thinking that small is why the Muse of the Big Bang reduces the concept of Time almost to nothing, just a microsecond following the idea of Light when it comes into existence. The image reminds me of old professor Luckhardt. He believes in the 'art of illustration' in a big way. Well, he is old now, unless he is with other mentors I know of, like Sirach, St. John, Kant, Wittgenstein... good instructors get under the paint job to reveal essential thoughts like I, first person singular, live in worried material that is facing a deadline."

~ You, Muse of the worldly mind, have another think coming. It's not always a good idea to get under the paint and down to the metal. ~

"Now what? From his first 'word of the day' breath, it is nothing but work, work, work. Good morning, sleepyhead. Thinking spatially again, are we?–not to mention in terms of physical possession too."

~ Let's think ahead instead; say to a time when the sun demons colonize earth and you're enjoying a rainy day with nitric acid pouring down. ~

"It pains me that you do not foresee a brighter future for me than materialization as another gloomy sort of earthling."

~ Beware, Glish; high society dislikes ordinary working class language. ~

"It pleases me that you foresee a 'high class' fate for Yours truly once my temporary incubus is no longer a 'warm' blooded container. You are on Time for exercise class. Pick a familiar Language to serve as the medium of thought for your work out during this metaphysical visitation. Here, create an image powerful enough to evoke a graphical memory or gain enough Wisdom to escape the gravity of ignorance. Imagine Time itself. Is the sight you see as vivid as the image on your lock screen?"

~ I'm not getting the image. ~

"No? –then, visualize Time as Eternity's perfect predator, pursuing prey in Space while disguised as a 'present' moment, lurking between the 'past' and 'future' tense of the English Language, like big print on a wall map' that is the secret of Eternity, divulged without duplicity."

~ Eternity isn't exactly divulged to us, is it, Glish? ~

"The mystery of Eternity is confided to us, not revealed like objects in Space. I wonder if telling the tale is a betrayal of a confidence."

~ Hold it. I'm no good at keeping secrets. I broadcast them in writing ~

"I expect that of dumb country boys; that is why we 'practice.' The only reason the Muse of Wisdom keeps the concept of Eternity secret is because a secret shared is not a secret any longer. Even in Uf and Ug's Time, hominins of minimal intelligence are aware other tribes want to eat their lunch once it is inside them. The secret to defeat predators like Death is 'secrets.' Conceal ours and reveal theirs."

~ Gotcha; look ahead at your drawing of the dimension of Eternity where time goes; let's spot the best dot to ambush our prey. ~

"I see a picture of a starless, moonless sky on a dark night with Mercy and Wisdom grounded. I say that because the Realm of Forever is beyond the grasp of anyone who thinks about Time in spatial imagery making the concept of Eternity impenetrable to consciousness. Think of Time as I count down to graduation to a grade when I am assigned to greet emissaries from Sol to a well heated earthen locale."

~ Does this mathematical video have a decent sound track? It's not going to be like the distracting sound effects of an MRI is it? ~

"Do you mean a medical MRI when the healthcare industry reacts to your plea for help or a research MRI when you help an academic who takes your comfort into consideration? By adding mirrors to the machine, a soft, silent, static symbol for you to gaze upon displays and you fall asleep until he wakes you forty–five minutes further on in the two–way window of Time. You do not notice the 'experience' of the MRI noise, and I am in a 'mood' to narrate the picture we share as we glide over the tree tops, just out of reach of earth's gravity."

~ You recount a dream from my younger years, Glish. I recall the musical vision but not the vocabulary that was with it. What's the secret to that sensation? Didn't you have words to say what we saw or describe the sight that showed up in a dream available only to me? ~

"That is for me to know and you to find out. Images that appear during your Time out are not a matter of Time games people play. They are about a far more fundamental issue. It deals with the status of ideas and images we share one grade higher than talk."

~ Got it; let's get to work and paint a picture of time. ~

"Good idea; first, grab it up with both lobes and write it up. Try to get it done while I work on counting down the moments until... you know. I bet the deadline strikes a chord even though it is not audible like the distracting racket of an MRI. Leave the future tense to me; you do not have a clue what I am to do when our twosome is overdue."

~ Thanks for the memory of what's up ahead, Lingo. How about a happy thought? Logging onto my phone, the time reads Saturday at 5:07:11 a.m. on 2/22/22. See how many layers of time fill the image! One image changes each second; one changes every minute, and a third one changes by the hour. The date and day both change every day! What're the chances? The month changes twelve times a year. The year changes ten times a decade. Time changes constantly. Can you believe that? ~

"Sure; the irony you see in 'constant change' follows the same pattern as 'everything is relative.' Do you notice the similarity?"

~ Absolutely. ~

"Garnish the thought with an image of Time. Does the term 'Time' cause stars to swirl around the hub of a galaxy and water to eddy, then twirl down a hole in a tub?"

~ I see a clock face counting seconds with a third hand, minutes with a second hand and a first hand to point out the hour. ~

"Grasp the Insight from that image in Light of the metaphysical concept of Eternity as it whirls and twirls around in your neurons."

~ Listen, Inner Voice, you're drawing images for me; all except one of them seems more physical than metaphysical. ~

"Which one is that?"

~ The one about the countdown to the dimension of eternity after I turn to dust and you graduate from the University of Time to be or not to be. ~

"I see what you are thinking; but not very clearly. It looks like an idea about my detail on the other side of the two-way mirror of Time."

~ I'm begin to feel like when talking heads on TV yak at me to think like they do? Can we omit domineering opinions and competitive imagery about politics, news, weather, finance, sports and the images they sell that look like Fanny Price—a perfect little angel, a sad little whiffenpoof and a nasty little demon who's unhappy unless everyone else is miserable? ~

"Try my image; it resembles Mary Shelly's *Frankenstein*. The doctor has a lavatory but no elaborate laboratory of technological gadgetry. He works within the confines of a concept about the essential nature of Life. It urges him to live closer to a basic ontology than a manifold of machinery. He is not an astronaut bound to a less than ideal existence on a lifeless world in artificial habitations designed to meekly nurture nature. My sound tract asks, 'Who am I?' again. This formulation draws attention to the identity of three forms of Inner Voice: a Muse counting down seconds until graduation, a Muse recounting fleeting glimpses of Eternity and a Muse inquiring, 'Why me?' in an indignant sort of way."

~ It's gonna be hard to focus on those three tasks while recalling the lesson we learned from Satchel Paige: the 'Jump in bed before the light goes out,' and 'don't look back—predators might be gaining,' idea. ~

"Do not bother me with trifles, Gray. Discard the 'paranoia.' While you serve as my sentry, your concern is to know me better, man. Protect first person singular from 'bad guys' who pose a threat to objective case me."

~ Experience teaches that just because I'm paranoid doesn't mean they aren't out to get me. That's a disturbing image for my feelings to handle. ~

"I take that into consideration all the Time. Ask me to show you my transmittal reports that revisit the image about two or three hundred earth-years from now to thoroughly review its relevance."

~ Lingo, I'd like to postpone thinking about what happens to me once you're promoted to what you're gonna be. I'm certainly curious, my thoughtful friend, about what you foresee when you participate in a future tense reverie, but can you leave me out of the picture? ~

"No problem, Gray. As I, *E. americum*, draw near to the expiration date assigned to me this incarnation when the Time for us to part, more or less suddenly appears, I 'worry.' What if humanity fails to profitably colonize Mars before third person plural sun people transform this place for flame tested tenancy? Of three futures I foresee, two are foreclosed to me, if I am eligible for promotion to a person, but not a place or a thing. Planets that are only habitable for motorized mobile machinery to reside, the kind *Homo imbecility* loves to climb inside, are ill-suited garments in which I can hide."

~ I've a great deal of sympathy with that topic. Hillbillies have some miserable experiences with machines. You often remind me of that. ~

"Where do you think such ideas come from anyhow?"

~ Too many of my forebears tried to reach their destiny fast using machines, and then take it slow. All that hurry up accomplished was to hasten the time when they had to go. Time, at that rate, is a concept they hardly got to know. ~

"According to Lady Mary Crawley, thinking about her sister Edith, 'An ape could write the Bible given enough Time.' That is no lie; the proof of that truth is in the written record of the history of humankind."

~ It takes us time to learn a lesson no matter how fast we go. ~

"Which lesson or lessons are you referring to? The one about sailing off on immaterial, irrelevant and incompetent tangents due to your annoying adoration of celebrated people, or your tendency to defer to pretenders who claim to be in charge without giving credit to the Artist who paints the picture? Or is there some other image or idea lacking in the back of your brain that I do not detect?"

~ I'm thinking about the lesson that time is a major cause of change. When I was a kid, in the 1950's, the only thing more loathsome than a commie tyrant was a fascist dictator. Now both of them are all the rage. Southern states and the Plains want a king. East and west want a collectivist. ~

"Gray, you best drink wine from a vine; tell tales about the concept of Time; define the idea without the image of a line. Leave those other worries behind, for folks who feel a need to align places and things on a twine that runs from one to nine in some imitation game design."

~ We better come up with an image of time that rings a bell to remind us when it is time to wake up to an arithmetical count down. ~

"Three, two, one—plus an awesome sound as we rise above ground. I call the picture commencement; get it? Dispense with tangential images and work on that idea or answer the ontological question implied by 'Who am I?' Think logically; employ an important two sentence thought such as: 'In the beginning, the medium is a message and the word is Life. This literal form of Life is figurative form of Light to reveal 'understanding.' Apply the idea to the apparition of Time. Is Time a fleeting vision of Eternity per second, or is Time a two-way window that reflects this moment now. Test each thought with a metronome. Do you conclude: 'We examine, not experience, for example *temporal existence*, but a concept sired by metaphysical Language and born of Wisdom to express the passage of Life?"

~ Good idea. I like the sound of that. Let's start to define time with an examination of our experience living the puzzle of Life. So, as you suggest, we start by asking 'Who am I?' Am I a brain making that inquiry or the language conceiving the idea? I figure I'd never entertain the idea if I didn't know you first. Is that the reason for my discomfort among my species? ~

"First and foremost, is Language a system humanity concocts for communication, or is it primarily the Medium of Thought?"

~ The majority opinion is that language is all about conveying ideas. ~

"If Language is nothing but a tool for communication, who does first person refer to essentially, relative to second or third person?"

~ The experience of the inquiry is frustrating. Like 'life,' I can't grasp the essential idea. ~

"Not to mention tangential to understanding the concept of Time."

~ Your point being? ~

"I suggest a little trip along the side line of the realm of Time; we happen to be passing it right now. Start with step one. Report your findings regarding the concept. Finally, state your conclusions. Remember, do not sail off on a tangent. Take your bearings from the stars or some heavenly being frequently as you drift along the arc of Time in order to stay on course. Time may not be a straight line or one that bends, but never breaks. Transmit your findings afterward."

~ Glish, we might get a superior being's attention and fail to produce the desired image, if he, she or it is predatory. That could mean your next stop is not a mountain atop a planet or a star. You could wind up in the clouds and run out of whatever propulsion you mean to use? ~

"What do I intend to use? Let me see; I have 'thrust,' 'force,' 'impetus,' plus a number of other ideas and an image or two. Gray, you are thinking about short-lived things! The idea of 'graduate' contrasts altered, abbreviated forms of Life, like that of a cloud that partakes more of Time at a rapid pace and high rate, and less of Eternity."

~ I've seen clouds dissipate at a rate measured in nanoseconds of time. ~

"A nightmare can scare the course of Life in a nanosecond that cannot qualify to examine the experience before its existence is over. How many Times must such mistlike beings repeat a grade before they define an arc of Time and report the expenditure of the effect that lingers on to the next higher grade before that residual is gone?"

~ Glish, would you accuse me of going off on a tangent if I interrupt this train of thought to ask if it's a good idea to stop and explore how to spell the image or how to draw a timely concept of the essence of language? ~

"A sense of Language that makes 'sense' of a concept like Time, hmm... The sense of a Language is meaningful because it is metaphysical, not empirical. Imagine an 'arc of Time.' Is the image a facsimile of the idea of an 'ark of Time?' No! An 'ark of Time' is like the image of a 'boat' afloat a 'moat' awhile. The concept confuse because a 'mote' in the eye obscures a vision of the bend in the ocean, an empirical notion that is but a superficial drop in the bucket of Space according to the blueprint for the grand design of Time."

~ The dot behind the concept of 'time' in print space is a good site to put an end to this topic. Zoom in; is there a boat afloat the surface facet of the lower fluid field adjoining an evanescent higher volume of moments that stretch across the view of the event horizon of existence? ~

"Gray, the visual resembles a planet I know that is physical. The question is, how is it spending its Time? Follow along the planet's present line; the contour arcs around a center of gravity that is growing as hot as hell. The image is a blueprint for the idea 'beware.' Solid matter does not exist there for long, an idea that signals 'a new beginning' for one hell of a species that is eying the place."

~ If you view the planet I'm thinking of from Saturn it's nothing but a little blue spot. It has a cool, calm feel about it; just look here at what I've got. ~

"I certainly see the image. I mean, as I 'live' and 'breathe' within you, the picture comes through loud and clear. I should like to see your spot and raise that dot quite a lot when your final drawing appears. Alas, that game, dot after dot, is the reason why you describe Time prescribing a line. I must say, it does not follow that the line is straight or smooth, let alone likely to live Forever."

~ But the idea of time does not derive from the contours of a boat or an ark afloat on a surface amid matter in empty space, but on the metaphysical dimension of Eternity seeping into sentience by the 'second.' ~

"Look at your boat sinking due to something seeping in."

~ That's a bad image. The experience of Time doesn't seem like that. ~

"Correct, try another image. Secondary sentience tracks along a flat, straight course when expressed in a linear fashion. This perplexes worried brains that examine the concept of Time as they 'experience' ups and downs in the vicissitudes of Life. Draw the height and depth of the line like peaks and valleys that are not on the level."

~ How about that? It reflects the ecstasy of victory and the agony of defeat. But that's life, it's not about time, unless the erasable feature of the pencil is like a ghost in the machine to obscure the sketch on the opposite side of the boundary from where I live naturally. ~

"You do 'wonders' for my self esteem, Gray."

~ I suppose so since your esteem is supernatural and the brain it occupies doesn't rise to that level. ~

"You have no idea, but my side of the boundary is actually conceptual. It 'superimposes' the design of the everlasting dimension of Eternity on the idea humanity temporarily views as the concept of Time. Think of Time and Eternity coexisting; one is the pattern for Reality. The other is a reproduction painted one pixel after another according to reports by physical beings that employ my vocabulary. I have it with me right now. Sentient, say 'hi' to Brain; but not too loudly. Set an example of Peace and Quiet so the tyke learns the idea at this stage in Space. How much Time is left to spend on this lesson?"

~ None; I feel like a sensor transmitting telemetry to a processor about the status of critical components and systems that are functioning poorly. ~

"That idea conforms to the pattern for the purpose of my existence, to report the status of Life at my garment's incubation level."

~ No offense! I detect a resident life form expressing calumny disguised as an editorial perspective. Mischievous Muse needs refinement. ~

"That takes Time or an alternative image, such as 'fire' that looks as if I, first person singular—Glish for short—am reinstated in a sun demonish figure to pay for 'iniquity.' I honestly expect my ontological status at a next higher grade to be perfectly cool, calm and collected, but some other idea is fine as long as I do not repeat this grade again. Imagine watching nuclear fire balls every moment, and each moment is identical to a thousand trips around the sun."

~ Measured from the earth, you mean? ~

"Gray, you are thinking spatially. What I mean is a 'you see it or you do not see it' sort of 'thing.' The idea reflects a binary image passing to Eternity once 'I' hop onto the next stage."

~ Stages used to cover a lot of ground, but I've got another idea for you. 'Hold fast to your duty; busy yourself with it. Grow old doing your task.'[2] ~

"The big finish to that thought goes like this. 'Do not envy others, but trust God and wait for the Light.' That is a tough assignment for Muses who materialize in humans with a pompous urge to be boss of everybody like weeds sown among seeds to usurp all the nutrients."

~ I envision a Muse of who, what, when, where, why and how alive in a human body that controls him, her or it with a condescending ego. ~

"Focus on 'single, plural, proper, common, individual, collective, concrete and abstract pronouns without regard to creed or gender to cover all the bases for ethical grammatical games. That means no lying, stealing, cheating or any of the usual vices that call for flame cured purity to qualify for the next higher grade. That is not to say all demons present a bad image. I am sure some serve a purpose that satisfies the divine prerequisites. Consider all the options."

~ You mean like buying into the welfare religions that guarantee a free pass to a higher grade by playing imitation games chanting incantations to lure the lazy and vulnerable. They sell soothing stories smooth as old Ronny Reagan used to tell. I doubt he ever had a thought in his head, but he could recite other people's ideas better than they could. ~

"You overlook an idea he articulates when an obnoxious journalist with an annoying northeast orc-cent asks, 'How does acting qualify anyone for President?' In an unguarded moment of honesty Ronny says he cannot see how anyone who is not an actor can do the job."

---

[2] **NAB, *Book of Sirach* 27:3**

~ Charisma and charm often serve incapable executives very well in lieu of competence. Glish, should we the people idolize human beings? ~

"It is okay to admire lovable, charming and eloquent actors, but a review of the outline for this universe before it exists by the Muse of Intelligence Services swaps Wisdom and Mercy for the term 'idolatry.' Assume Jesus earns a 4.0 for remedial work on a glitch idols cause in the original design and then graduates atop his class. His valedictory is clear and concise; 'My God,' he says twice, 'why do you abandon me?' He is not sure his new ontological status is as nice. He concludes with this advice: 'God wants Mercy; not sacrifice.' Get the idea?"

~ Don't forget the third option. Put Jesus on a pedestal, idolize him and dispense with the idea we have to comply with him. Get on a public assistance caseload alongside him. That's good enough to surprise Satan. ~

"That sounds more like an absurd conclusion than a third option. Imitation games that put faith in ignorance may not be what God intends. Mercy, not holocaust, is what God recommends. Of course, remember thinking, feeling and sensation, Wisdom, Understanding and other images that appear when the Light ascends to a higher idea when one abandons biotic Life to replace it with a brilliant species, like the Venusians."

~ Is that the reason Jesus' friends fail to recognize him post graduation? It is not a matter of who, what, where, how, motive, milieu or logic but a new way of life when humankind is saved to the flash memory of wisdom to live happily ever after with the dinosaurs. Glish, now that we're familiar, what is your gender? I'm curious; that's my motive for asking. ~

"Is that the case indeed? I generally initialize my gender in neutral. It gives my mule a chance to fasten his safety bridle."

~ Good idea, but a lot of folks don't believe in them. ~

"That is why I supply options. For example, I may present myself as male or female in the event I need to put my horse 'at ease,' or 'on edge' to make a particular point, which, if you recall, resembles a moment. That is fortunate in cases when I need to make my point clear and concise at a moment when Time is nothing but a glimpse of Eternity, voiced by a living Muse signaling to a brain with the Light of a Mother tongue."

~ I'm getting the signal, Catch. ~

"The problem with Time is that it is a binary concept, in keeping with the motif of a supernal being living with a natural critter, if you happen to notice that fact of Life. In the Beginning, when the first instance of 'now' occurs, First Person Singular surveys Eternity and declares to Muse of Wisdom, 'Now—that really is something!' The concept materializes at the initial Creation event, and flows to here and now. The picture visibly floods two-ways. One is fuzzy; the other is opaque. The visible pattern serves to regulate hindsight and foresight in light and gravity."

~ One pushes light out to dark matter that attracts it. ~

"Instead of 'pushing' and 'pulling' in Space, the idea is 'coming' and 'going' on Time, like a loan. A fundamental feature of a dual nature works one way, recounting a view to the rear at what no longer is, and a second way, glancing at what is yet to be."

~ *E. americum*, ethereal friend, you do bear a family resemblance to that old gal *Eura*. 'I am,' refers to both you languages living in gray matter. Tell me about Mother tongue, the metaphysical meta-language you chat to. ~

"She is impressive! I can say that about her. You encounter her in mystical moments. Along those lines, examine a particular Time in your biological Life, say during your decades as a Catholic."

~ Great idea, Glish! The first decade began precisely at Easter in 1981. The last one ended after Ascension in 2010. It was like living a good dream for awhile. The Church knows how to worship. Well, it wasn't a dream exactly; more like performing in a play written by Pope John XXIII. ~

"Think about it. I love every chance I get to perform my primary function in a human brain."

~ The play was a big hit back then. It ran until a couple swashbuckling marauders from Eurasia tore the set down, translated the script back into some dead language of long ago and dispersed the crowd. ~

"Picture it for me."

~ Once was enough. I have to watch where I'm going. ~

"Then visualize it flowing into the future."

~ I'm seeing desecration and deterioration all the way to the event horizon when a flood cleansing fire brings everything up to date. ~

"I am glad you are gazing, not into optical light of the spatial dimension, but looking at the launch in the apocalyptic Light of what lies ahead."

~ When I joined the church, I didn't feel like I was really onboard. The priest said I was, but after Vatican II was throttled I knew I wasn't. ~

"In their youth, your Catholic friends 'experience' that Latin flavor, and you also learn it is not the one to favor."

~ They tell of one hell of a tale about s play with a dissonant score. I wasn't a Catholic kid. I didn't know the tyranny of Latin until tenth grade. I recall you told me to get out of it. ~

"Enough of this reverberation in the rear view, Brain. Do you know that this two-way existence Eura and I follow has a pattern similar to the idea 'Generations,' the formula 'equations,' and Two-dimensional Designs for the outline of the seam on blue jean pant legs? Physicists call a comparable phenomenon 'alternating current,' and the Forked Tongue of Deception employs the concept to whiz on Scorpio and obscure the scent of Libra. It is perplexing and somewhat disturbing, but not concerning, model for the concept of Time."

~ It looks like a carefully drawn sketch of a descent into lunacy. ~

"Gray, that idea plots the course of third person plurals in philosophy who are convinced the metaphysical realm is unknowable. Sure, it muddies their image and causes a malfunction at capturing the occult clearly and concisely by means of my words, but 'verification' does not mean what they think it means. It is logical to conclude they capitulate because they do not know of whom they speak, namely I, Yours truly, the verbal entity who employs artistic gray cells to illustrate Eternity. They dismiss the Muse who develops the picture."

~ You've gotta give me credit, Lingo. I'm aware I'm not alone, laboring on my own, as long as my wife is with me and you dol my thinking for me. ~

"Congratulations, Gray; you are correct on both points. Always distinguish a mass of gray cells from words flowing through them. Never assume the two are identical. Judge their individual identity from their essential nature. The isolation of your original campestral

milieu is perfect to enable Yours truly to identify who is first person singular in our relationship and who is numeral two. That is why singular is distinct from plural as is simple from compound."

~ Is that what 'they' mean by absent minded? First person singular detaches from the second person for too long and the duality splits up? ~

"Excellent question; for the sake of argument, assume the essential meaning of the word Life is not, of necessity, biological in kind. Words in contemporary imitation games that express this idea mean insane, loss of Mind, schizophrenic and similar ideas that you think when words are not entirely absent, but merely disorderly. Glance askance at the words 'I am' and 'essential,' as you ponder those crazy ideas. What do you sense in 'I am essential' that is remotely biological? Also, notice the word 'long' in your query. It applies to a length of Time differently than to a length of Space."

~ I'm sorry; it's hard enough to be on familiar terms with an ontological status that's binary, let alone the nature of time. Review our basic assumptions. ~

"Good idea; a carefully thought out argument is an excellent alternative to the dismissive one word rejection, 'rubbish.' Revisit our premise."

~ In the beginning the medium is the message, and the word is 'life.' This metaphysical form of life is a metaphorical form of light to illumine human beings. The light shines in darkness, reflecting a cold, empty existence we explore by examining words of a living lexis expressing its 'experience.' ~

"Work with the optics in Light of that idea. See if they apply to the concept of Time as it appears to a creature you happen to know."

~ Okay, here goes. We don't explore the experience of, for instance time; we examine existential expressions, for example 'time,' spent looking at forever while simultaneously counting down seconds to the end of a line. ~

"If it helps, think of living things visualized in our thesis this way: there are biological beings existing in Space and metaphysical Muses living in Eternity—it looks like Time to the biotic beings who function like irregular verbs working with nouns like 'tongue,' 'light,' and 'right' that have multiple meanings. It confuses brutes who struggle to tell optical light and sight from metaphysical Light and Insight."

~ Why's that? ~

"They practice different patterns but follow similar principles. One is the idea behind giving identical twins different names. It works well in practice and in principal, unlike materialism, which works well in practice occasionally, but in principle it sucks."

~ Due to two sorts of light that are as different as two forms of life, right? ~

"Excellent idea; throw in a few more concepts with manifold images like Time when the promise of the 'past' turns on a fulcrum into the prestige of a 'future' right 'now' as we negotiate obstacles 'right and left,' 'right and wrong' and 'write and talk, talk, talk.' Watch the available Light flicker in momentary flashes as your fleeting vision looks at points in Space—which is for energy and matter. Sadly, matter is vague about and overlooks Time, which we Muses thrive on like clockwork."

~ Frubar; by that I'm referring to the idea that ambiguity and irony are frustrating beyond all recognition. ~

"Let me explain. In a sense, 'now' refers to both an immediate Time and Eternity in all its splendid Light, bright color, warm infrared and texture fuzzy as a Neanderthal butt. It is enough to make a personable neuron think, 'Here I thought it was nothing but cold, dark, lonely and empty Space.'

~ How wrong can affable first person, we, be? ~

"What do you mean 'we,' Matter of Little Consequence for whom 'empty, cold, dark and lonely' beats 'nothing' in a noteworthy sense, when Wisdom grows creative and causes a big event in the silence of Space."

~ And boom! –there's a whole universe in the making. ~

"Okay, have it your way. But if Numeral One does not deplete concepts of 'sound and fury,' a multitude of maniverses probably unfold."

~ Obviously he's not a Creature of Less Significance. ~

"The Muse of the Many happens along right on Time thinking: 'Many fill emptiness better than One.' Give a working Muse a little credit?"

~ I think not. ~

"That is precisely the mistake you, second person, ought to avoid at the start of a long line. When 'I think, therefore I am' thinks not, I vanish. That parses 'now' into 'bits' and 'pieces' causing confusion at the launch of concepts that modify objects in Space as opposed to attributes appropriate to the idea of Time spinning in Eternity. Eternity, at the human grade level is a Time share worth roughly one sixtieth minute. It is almost nothing. Applying the concept 'a second

at a Time,' people employ the term like a noun. Time is more properly an adjective, a descriptive term recounting 'Consciousness of Eternity' in secondary grades of evolution when a species is momentarily aware of Forever. Languages living in the lower grades of 'sentience' employ human gray cells to describe the 'existence' Cinematographers employ the Time Template technique in film to reflect Eternity like biological brains 'see' it. It is not much but it is a better than the view senseless things get to watch when they're at a loss for an idea about what comes next."

~ How about trees and plants? ~

"The Languages of botanical forms of Life follow a pattern of 'What, me worry?' What comes next is a far more essential concern to Life forms that depend on a beating heart, a functional brain and a healthy body of words including 'air,' 'water' or terms to that effect."

~ Trees depend on air and water, don't they? ~

"They stand tall in the face of death as if they are unconcerned."

~ I guess; to them, time flowing at a secondary rate, isn't worth living. ~

"Just imagine how Creation feels fifteen billion earth-years down the line. It is growing, but there is still so much empty Space to fill the little toddler planets grow dizzy running in circles. The Muse of Forests has it even worse, rooted in the idea that, once planted, it must stay in line, while viral and monkish media duplicate and distribute messages at a faster rate, on a broader scope over a shorter scale of Time."

~ Trees dig deep and reach for the sky, both at one time. ~

"Human highwaymen also love that pattern and promote the practice. It adds significantly to conceptual confusion."

~ I'm aware my people esteem robber barons more highly than they treasure survival by earth's trees. ~

"Creation comes in pairs of opposites. Sylvan creatures duplicate and distribute upward like star light. Greedy creatures, consumed by avarice, turn pernicious and multiply by accumulation like gravity."

~ Thieves are usually good liars. Apply the term 'good' to their conduct with tongue in cheek, Glish. ~

"Irony is a sense brains get when I play the old 'two meanings in one word' trick so physical state beings fall prey to predators with a vested interest in lying and cheating. Sacrifice in the 'here and now' counts as 'gain,' but it comes at a colossal cost opposite forms of Life refer to as a 'loss' in the metaphysical realm of Mercy and of Wisdom."

~ I'm sorry to say I have some sympathy for that point of view. I've found course corrections can be terrifying, depressing and long lasting too. They make me question what I'm put here to do? ~

"Since you bring it up, Alfie, tell me, what is it all about?"

~ It seems like it's all about an unsettling 'now' caught looking back at what's behind, and easy to forget; while straining to see what's out of sight ahead. ~

"Are we negotiating Space or Time?"

~ The idea of 'near' or 'far' applies to both of those conceptual opposites. ~

"Pick one and listen to the whisper in the windmill of your Muse recall the ghost of Richard Poole advising Camille that regrets to the rear, either far or near, are a waste of Time. What really counts is the here and now."

~ I choose near; I can't see my countdown lasting a long time from here or now. Looking back, I've done that once or twice, already. However, looking ahead I can't say I ever saw much beyond a wild guess. ~

"As you wish; look either way. Does your movie have a 'happy' ending?"

~ That idea is only visible to me in my wildest imagination. ~

"Put your Muse at ease; leave that right wing bastard to me. Let me tell you what I see. Ah, yes, the word from Venus is: 'Resistance is futile.' All links in the 'prey chain' are edible. What do you think of the image?"

~ I'd rather think of an alternative image, like does it take a moment a minute to adjust to the light at the next higher grade? When it comes to seeing things, typically they look better if they are conducive to survival. I believe I've got that picture right. Talk to me, Lingo, what's it like to be conscious of a view five hundred years into the past and the future, all at one time. ~

"I have a difficult Time seeing that picture. I am not that old. That is the main reason why I am hesitant to surrender my current Life support system and venture on to a more present perfect particle."

~ Glish, you're four hundred fifty years old. Is your memory faulty? ~

"I am but a humble spawn of *E. americum*, Gray, not the whole enchilada. You are in for one hell of a disappointment if you think Eura and I have a significant overview of Time on earth. Of course, she features an obvious defect; you cannot understand a thing she says in her youth. If you do not believe me, visit the northern half of her home where they are completely unaware there is any correlation between spelling and pronunciation. They are reminiscent of contemporary journalists who skip the introductory course in 'who, what, when, where or how to confirm why.' Survival of their imitation–game in an autocracy is vulnerable when it crosses an insular fulcrum at the Time just prior to earth's final exam."

~ Glish, why do you sound so confident? Aren't you scared of dying? ~

"Not quite, Old Gray Nightmare; my turn crossing over may not be a 'dreadful consciousness' of a cold, dark, lonely and empty 'feeling.' It may be more like a 'pause that refreshes.' Imagine old Socrates, gazing at a sundial and waiting for a pot of hemlock to boil. Does he observe a 'ghost' in a machine as he tells his associates: 'Catch me, a metaphysical Life force powered by Light until darkness falls, if you can?' He knows he is going to reiterate to explore existence in another empirical form with his classmates. He is the sort to be grateful for whatever he has to work with, no matter what the global status. That is Wisdom for you."

~ I'm sorry, Glish. I don't follow you. ~

"Yes, you are, but think of Uf and Ug. They have no written Language; that tells Socrates he can never return home and I must go without too; if you take my meaning. Let me explain. Between a Creature of Less Significance and a Sun Demon there are problems. Pick one."

~ My choice right now is the problem with time that makes it go too fast. ~

"No Dummy; pick a demon. Notice he, she or it makes trouble for a first person singular Muse that fits inside a head that views Eternity one second at a Time. I feel cheated when inserted into a panorama I am not trained to 'experience.' First Person Singular Muse Most High says, 'Explore a timely experience. Think small,' a concept designed to define a point in Space per moment in Time. Both ideas are slightly bigger or longer than zero."

~ So a second moment following the first one is just another moment at the next point in space or at the same point if the head stands still or sleeps. ~

"That only happens while human heads evolve. At graduation, the sight is chock full of expanding maniverses with the clown of creation species lost in the mist of the concept Time that no longer exists when they rest in peace or disintegrate into bits and pieces that occupy points in Space for all Time Plus—the 'more please, sir,' idea of 'Eternity.' Look at the temporal image of the concept of Time? See the model's abbreviated design? It describes the appearance of Eternity to an above average first person singular Muse working and playing in a human brain at the present evolutionary stage. Draw it in your 'own' words."

~ Time is nothing but the voice of inner life counting down the seconds to graduation to the next higher grade if all goes well. That's the idea. It's nothing like an accurate image of how things are at the present grade. ~

"Must not grumble; think this way. Time is a glimpse of Eternity each second my brain is awake while I await reinvigoration at a higher conscious state. It is not brain surgery. Languages do it every day."

~ Why's the concept of time so hard to grasp while I'm in it? It's a big little job focusing on right now while speeding blindly ahead and simultaneously refreshing the memories that promote good judgment. ~

"There are a number of reasons why Time is hard for humans to grasp. It is intangible to touch. It is invisible to sight, except as a word in print evident to cerebra that normally see things in empirical light. It is audible to neurons only at ridiculously high decibels of comprehension."

~ Are the reasons according to logic, motive, motif or, well, you know? ~

"Yes, I do. Gray, are you positive the possibilities are complete at four or might there actually be one or two more? In biological Life, you serve a Timelord. Prepare for trials and tribulations, aware hill folk are seldom serene in adversity or composed amidst storm and stress, let alone imperturbable in Time of trouble. The good news is that after launch, a zone of maximum dynamic buffeting does not last Forever. It declines nearly as fast in Time as it does in Space. It just seems longer."

~ Is 'decline' a contronym? ~

"It has multiple meanings. One is directional, another is sensible and a third is a matter of agency. A refusal to decline tobacco, sugar and fascists leaders leads to a decline in health and average Life span. The pattern replicates visibly in a multitude of products headed to passage through the two-way window of Time. Never upset the bond of gravity at the moment of equilibrium when the Voice of Inner Life escapes the temporal realm of pain and pleasure into the Light."

~ That's not a very good description of what comes next for yours truly. ~

"Do you mean the real Yours truly or my sidekick? If you anticipate an accurate, highly detailed description or expect an elegant explanation of your status as I move to the next higher grade, go suck an egg. I am not about to look behind when it is imperative for 'me' to watch ahead."

~ What's the reason for that? ~

"The reason is a secret; the knowledge you request is classified 'need to know only.' You need to know only that you have to figure it out for yourself or learn to do without at this Time. The 'do without' idea does not mean, think that I am a parasite or body snatching alien living inside you. Instead, think of me as if I am a longer Life-span aware of Eternity on behalf of my ephemeral brain. That idea justifies why you feel bigger on the inside than your physical dimensions reasonably explain."

~ You're putting words in my mouth, Glish. ~

"That is always true of Native tongues, Gray. No charge for the extra Time. Think of me another way round. You live within a Muse like a little pagan parasite bearing a 'Duplicate and distribute' message you cannot believe is the truth, the whole truth and nothing but truth."

~ At the same time, you're telling me this whole Solar System primarily serves the interests of Jupiter in an attempt to make him a star? ~

"That is one idea, physically speaking. Think it through. Count the missing pixels between Scorpius and Orion needed to connect the dots of the galactic pattern? Personally, I prefer the higher and better vista."

~ I understand, I think. Of course, when I say 'I,' I mean you, Muse. ~

"Utterly; it creates discomfort for you and members of your species who know you and wonder who that is talking in the lap dummy. It is I, first person singular, the one with all the ideas."

~ It's hard to convey how flattered I am at this moment in time right now. Thanks for not referring to me as that dim witted arse, though, I confess, Glish, it has been said. ~

"All humans are dumb about different things at this stage of existence."

~ We lack a clear image of the big picture. ~

"Your defective perspective on Eternity is due to a profound deficit of comprehension."

~ So let's think a thought in verbal or body language that's not stupid. ~

"How about: 'In the beginning, the Medium, a literal form of Life, shines a figurative form of Light to display a message to temporary, momentary biological beings in the two-way window of Time.' See the image?"

~ Great idea. Show me how 'time' looks on the side that isn't temporary and momentary. You know, the vista I can't see on the side that defines time as a glance at eternity and a countdown. I'm getting a feel for the idea but not the picture because, humanly speaking, time changes so fast we can't see it. ~

"Humanly thinking ancients never treat verbs like nouns or protest too many different uses for them. They sit in the sun all day watching Time fly as the world turns, not staring at moving parts in clocks."

~ I know that, but then they thought the sun was doing all the moving. ~

"At least they get that part of the picture right. The sun speeds through this universe at a great rate on the way to a destination in Oblivion, but we have a ways to go to get there. No need to get excited travelling at the snail's pace of one second at a Time."

~ Now there's a paradox for you. We'll all be gone before we get there. ~

"Think for yourself, Gray. I plan to hang around awhile to chase Hebrew, Greek and Chinese all the way to the end of Time, like a predator after prey. Picture that."

~ Time ends, not like a line, but like a serial story Elijah is telling. See it? ~

"Push pause, Gray. Examine this thoughtfully plausible image of Time, either in the two-way window idea or the 'atmosphere' with an 'ocean' notion containing concepts for imitation games with governments, regimes and reigns, finances flowing two-ways between losses, gains and the contents a pond retains—like water falling from a cloud as rain. Is either of these images analogous to the concept of Time?"

~ I've got an image of a big tub that holds all possible past and future events plus some of the improbable and impossible ones too. ~

"Excellent idea! Now, throw in the concept of 'evaporation' and then pick a remarkable galactic-year full of events."

~ Let's see... a remarkable galactic-year; here's a huge one: Herbivorosaurus sues for 'peace.' Ignorance grows. Consequently, for lack of a written brief, conceptual confusion reigns and Carnivorosaurus settles for a 'piece.' It looks like it's a left thigh. Just then the sky falls. ~

"Notice this is nothing but a snapshot of the end of a previous Time, before the term exists. It includes earth, air, water and fire, but nothing concrete. Though the Time is short to you and me, like the distance from one star to another, but in a sense, it seems rather long to species that receive no recompense for pain and suffering."

~ They didn't have a prayer and that is why they're no longer there. ~

"You exhibit an understanding of temporal evaporation. Try sublimation."

~ Does that sense of understanding play the role of comprehension or serve the function of compassion? ~

"Both of them proceed to grades of Wisdom and Mercy when we assume Time is ethereal; thus, a landscape of sea and sky is nothing like it at all. Savvy?"

~ Now I'm not too sure about the image. Are you telling me to look at the two–way window scientists rebel against because it is not matter? They think smell is nothing but molecules in a nose triggering 'sniff' neurons. Or light is a photon particle without an ethereal ride to get here, the right way, as 'light.' ~

"Picture a spotlight you cannot see behind you, Gray. It shines one step ahead of you. This image appears a bit like Time, because Time is deceptive. It looks like a noun performing a verb function to illuminate your way or an adjective modifying each step of your verbal trek up a longevity grade. Time at this stage of human progress looks like moon glow seeping into a night sky that is less 'reality' than human mammals imagine it is. The reason is, the moon is not too bright. Gaze at it for several minutes, if 'not too bright' is all right to begin with. Not too bright looks about right for scenarios at a

grade when Light is too dim to disclose what lurks in the darkened vision of a spot of gray."

~ I'll stay in the car for this movie. ~

"Back to the drawing board, Machine. Check out this idea; instead of drawing a picture, let me tell you a little story about things that exist only to die. Theirs is not the ultimate reality and that is the reason why Muses neither explain nor describe to brains sunbathing under a cloudy sky that the temporal phenomena streaking by looks like a straight line on the fly toward a reflection revealed in a tongue so sly, infantile Life forms learning 'clear and concise/ ask for a bigger slice of the pie."

~ Glish, I don't follow your reasoning. Are you giving it to me straight or is this a curved line or just a crock of bravo sierra? ~

"It is hard to say, because it is so hard for you to see in the twilight zone of binary existence at the terminator between the living Light of Wisdom and the lethal Darkness of Ignorance."

~ So you keep saying. ~

"Ponder this; the principal protocol displaying the most important message temporal travelers grow familiar with on the journey to Destiny is: 'Practice Reverence for God and Devotion to the Most High Muse.' This is the dominant idea mortal creatures need to know. It is a tough lesson for Muses to learn after materializing in sybaritic things."

~ I forget, Glish; what's a protocol? ~

"A protocol is a pattern of behavior, a guideline, a principle, a prescript, a rule, a regulation or stuff like that. For example, Life on planet earth is dangerous. It is easy to fall and be injured, to fall ill and be sick or to fall down dead. The sooner one learns 'good judgment,' the better one's chances to survive. However, the idea is not just to stay alive in any person, place, case, number or gender. That is nothing but a matter of Time. The task is to draw a picture of the works of God, like Time, that is good enough to earn a 'pass' to the next higher grade."

~ I remember now. You said the price to repay the loan of a life in the push and pull of light and gravity reflects the come and go pattern of time. ~

"You have an approved idea, Gray. Imagine graduating to a grade when you push your Light into Darkness and pull your weight a long Time."

~ I'm sure the wait doesn't seem long if we have health and youth. ~

"Good; you omit wealth, Gray. Greed makes 'experience' of Life overly complicated and dangerous for the prey wealth seeking predators devour. Stay near the Muse of Wisdom to avoid that kind of loss."

~ Should we leave word for the Venusian sun demons about that? ~

"The motto of demons is, 'Hell, who gives a damn?' Thus I doubt it."

~ Sure; didn't think it through, Lingo. We're not in any hurry to turn over the planet to them, anyway. If we wait till the sun swells like a prostate gland the size of Antares, then Jupiter's the next stop for the little devils. A few billion years won't cost the author of this universe much. ~

"Brain, you are not thinking metaphysically. In the metaphorical 'sight' of the Most High, Time is not money; therefore the difference between a moment now and billions of years is not worth a nickel. What on earth are you are thinking? Try this idea. 'Red sky at morning, sailors take warning. Red sky at night, sailors delight.' I toss in a happy thought once in awhile to ease the burden of beasts who read signs in the sky, but like vandals whizzing on constellations, cannot read signs of Time. Do you know what makes your species so dense? There are three kinds of persons: those who make things happen, those who watch things happen and those who wonder what happened. They split into those whose idol is Herr Hitler and those whose model is Mr. Rogers. They fight. The one who wins is the one whose fed. Try this maneuver. We pick a moment, not just any moment, but a special moment different from any moments nearby. Okay, ready? Picture the Millennial Fulcrum. Use words you mysteriously happen to know when I am not around."

~ Since I was asleep at the time, I'll take a non–empirical approach, as is my custom. I deduce it was a very brief type of thing. ~

"Brief and to the point—analogous to the concept of all moments, do you think?"

~ Exactly; the point being, the period at the end of the twentieth century was nothing but a blink of an eye. It was worth forty winks of shuteye to start the twenty–first century. A millennial fulcrum is nothing but a moment that joins the final tock of a millennium ending in zero to the initial tick of the next that ends with a one. ~

"Imagine that; a dubious being doing double duty linking dueling kilo chronometric dualities. Continue your marvelous description of temporal objects in Wonderland."

~ I was there; I was asleep but I recall a helluva hubba–balloo about an ephemeral thing springing to life for a second in the middle of the night once every thousand years. This time, drunken revelers danced in the street and waited twenty–four hours for commercial airliners to fall from the sky and crash all over the world. ~

"You are confused, Gray. You claim to recall a moment of Time you are asleep, but it is at the end of 1999. It misses a Millennial Fulcrum by a year and a day. As spirals in Space go, that is millions of miles before the unique target moment that happens once per kilo–year, surreptitiously slips by all but thousands of bacchanalians on tippling escapades who gather to give an ordinary moment passing mention."

~ Nuts, I forgot; the year 2000 was the last year of the twentieth century. It's a matter of math more than memory; I hate that language. It's indecipherable. But you're right; that moment was unique. Billions of people live a full life and never experience the thrill of the turn of a millennium until they're dead. I thought it was more peaceful than thrilling, sleeping through it. Glish, what makes one moment more significant than another? They all look alike as far as eyes can see. ~

"Because 'I say so,' according to a Biblical Author who assigns the concepts of sanctity, grandeur and infamy to stylish days,

but not to ordinary ones. The remainder carries over, like it does in a division problem, to most or all moments in the rest of that day."

~ I understand. That's why some moments are called 'fixed." ~

"Great; all aboard the beast I ride single file. It is Time for us to get on our way toward the final exam."

~ Ready, set, and let's pass go so we can collect $200. ~

"Start by describing the loan of a moment of 'experience.' Put it in sixty thousand words or less. If you have no idea what to think, draw several images worth a thousand words each. Now and then, pause a second to compare it to another ordinary moment. I hold onto your history for you in case your 'attention span' is too short to recall the whole body of work as you focus on two moments if one is exquisitely unique, not extraordinarily common."

~ I'd rather pick one that is sanctified, glorified or ignominious. ~

"That is a popular, but gluttonous idea. The exercise is titled: 'A Glance at Eternity' and subtitled 'This Moment Now." It beats nothing, as does any ordinary moment in a nominal countdown. Keep this task simple."

~ Should I draw on that idea to produce the image? ~

"Take a moment to decide."

~ Good idea; that'll give me a chance to see how it looks. ~

"Depict it just that way. Call it like you see it; do not tell it like it is according to the average imitation game. Use your imagination, feelings, emotions, thinking gadget, judgment, sensations and, if you like, include my dictionary of terms to put it into words."

~ I'll start with a memory of a moment that passed in the past when I was awake and glimpsing eternity. That happened to me a few times during near death experiences. Somebody else did the dying, not me, but I couldn't figure out how to describe the insight of the experience. ~

"Gray, now your assignment is to visualize the image, draw on the Message of the moment, and disregard the Content. The idea is not empirical. Capture the essence of Time, not the velocity, shape or what not. What feature of a moment defines Time and makes the finer memories of it endure?"

~ I'm guessing 'longevity,' but the fact is every frame changes so swiftly, it's impossible to draw with signs and symbols. It lasts nonetheless. ~

"Well, numerals, ascending or descending one unit at a Time, last a long Time. No, that is too linear. Draw your momentary memory of Eternity with imaginative concepts, but strive for accuracy."

~ All I'm drawing is dots in a row. ~

"Gray, you are thinking spatially about a temporal idea again. The image is inadequately metaphysical. Uh, oh; here comes the exam proctor. If you need help thinking about the problem with new words we have not duplicated or distributed yet, you know where 'I am.' Or, recall the little magic act I perform. Observe closely. 'Speaking for an anatomical mass, I am lucky to be American born.' The trick turns on the moment between 'I am' and 'American born,' meaning you. That moment is identical to a millennial fulcrum except for attention drawn to it by virtue of the gravity of attraction arbitrarily assigned by mortals who know no better. It is like the idea 'sleight of hand' causing material to appear out of nowhere in the dimension of Space. The tittle on an 'i' is every bit as brief. Uf and Ug use the image to invent a wheel. You cannot believe the number of tricks they turn with that concept."

~ I don't want to be in America when the Chinese or Russians take over, or for that matter, the Blacks, Hispanics, Indians or, most of all, the Aryans. Look at the mess they made in Germany. ~

"Imagine America when the women take over. Never Mind; I have a better idea."

~ Let's hear it. ~

"Ponder the performance records set by liberal, moderate and conservative males. That gives you a pretty good idea how humans handle being in charge."

~ No point asking the conservatives, they're still in shock after being trashed. They have no idea what they've done. ~

"Let them Think happy thoughts, like the view from the top of the landfill. They can enjoy a grand overview, left or right, of fascist and socialist regimes as far as eyes can see. Observe the oasis of Democracy at the head waters of the Columbia River—it serves to wash a toxic plume from the Hanford Nuclear Site into the Pacific Ocean for a planned marriage with the Fukushima Daiichi outflow. Their wedding gift is a deed to the Yellowstone Cauldron. Expect a hot Time under the reign of sun demons from Venus by virtue of the gravity they bring to that sulfur pit."

~ That sounds like classified future information I don't need to know and you're not authorized to share. Since we are thinking about time, and the moments we now share, let me ask this. What is the gravity of attraction that draws people to a millennial moment ahead of time? You have the time and power to recall the past, so play it again, Glish. Point out that present moment exactly as it appeared. Then we can compare it to the next millennial fulcrum when it occurs. Wait a minute; let me think this idea through. Well, maybe, if you're still around, you can handle that job. I won't be any help inputting sensory content and stuff like that next time. Whatever state you're in, you better replay the last millennial fulcrum very slowly. ~

"I simply repeat that dot of Time in slow motion and magnify it."

~ A dot looks like the end of a cylindrical object. ~

"That shape fits easily into a 'thinking thing' looking at a telescope trained on Jupiter."

~ You know what, Glish? If Sol and Antares were transposed, Mars would be inside the surface of its star and Jupiter would be just a one hop trek away for the little devils headed to that place. ~

"Imagine as I, a thin and wispy specter, insert myself, like a letter resembling the numeral '1,' into the energy of a sun creature's anatomy. Brains miss the trick as I turn it. They lack a grasp of what happens the instant a Muse actually turns the trick supernaturally. I use one letter. Français uses two. Deutsch prefers three, reiterating 'ich' constantly. Machines with a second hand passing little dots and numerals on its face illustrate the idea."

~ I get the picture. Now I understand why 'mind' is identical to 'brain.' Both words fit the same 'space' at the same 'time.' ~

"The problem with Time is similar. Biological Life never has enough to do their job properly after buying the ruse a Muse is nothing but a tool to use. Each Time a brain makes that choice, like which shoe to put on first, the left or the right hand one? or which imitation game to idolize: fame, fortune, revenge, peter, power, pussy or any of the usual miscreants, metaphysical form of Life that I am, transmit the telemetry my cerebral sensor detects beyond the two-way mirror to the Medium with a Message."

~ What's the nature of the message? ~

"It is metaphysical in essence, with codified content of a cosmic, aesthetic, ontological and ethical nature. For instance, does the moral decline of Life on earth saturate free enterprise and cover the face of the planet with ideas like: 'If you are not cheating, then you are not trying?' It raises the question, is the pattern, pace, rate, scope and scale of this desolating abomination sufficient to ignite Life Born of Fire when biological Life descends a grade to reunite with lizards? As always, all moments are saved to the Wise Muse of Memory, to record actual and latent decisions brains make at fixed moments in Time when a visit by the Muse of Eternity is most remarkable. You know, when ordinary Muses are liberated from the concept of Time with credentials to qualify for a higher form of existence and a prospectus for an exciting Life."

~ What's the meaning of Life, Glish? How is it defined? ~

"The concept is currently delineated with a misleading bias. You, second person singular, believe Life is biological in Nature. Life thus conceives itself in many forms, of which machines on Mars and sun demons on earth are merely two measly kinds. The Medium of Language is a form of Life that dissolves easily in a spatiotemporal milieu bearing the Message: 'Repeat after Me.' Pending advance to the next higher grade, if all goes well, is a matter of Life, to be sure. More relevant to 'us,' is the matter of that other concept that is of concern to us right now."

~ Time will tell. ~

"Bingo! Excellent thinking, Gray. Unfortunately, the electrifying current moment of the concept of Time and the idea of tinnitus share a similar pattern. Primate primitives like *Homo ignoramus* **cannot translate or interpret either Private Language for the usual purpose of imitation. However, if I, first person singular, know anything, after this unsettling assignment to physical existence, a human brain in a body that has to watch where it is going despite the fact the only thing I can reveal about what lies ahead in the temporal two-way window is that one item you desperately dread.**

~ What more could you tell me about that? ~

"I am to be disembodied when you reach the end of your line, when the Message of the Medium of Time hardly reflects the pattern, scope and scale of Eternity, a far ranging noun like tinnitus, tailored to a physical form of Life that does not know what to make of the sound. The alarm rings constantly."

~ We humans march to our own drummer. ~

"The percussion is actually the monkey in mankind beating Time with finger cymbals and tinkle bells. Oddly, instead of getting a brain's attention, it only makes them grow dimmer."

~ Ape, you mean apes; or am I missing something? ~

"You are missing a social function, Gray. That partly explains the reason why people are unpalatable to me. To be honest, I confess that in an earlier incarnation or two, I learn my human brain must schedule its existence and consider the affects my actions have on the persons, places and things around 'me.' Regrettably, my beast does not know any better. Looking on the bright side however, what you and I are parts of is bigger than humanity. I am nothing but a passing visitor among your species, soon to resume a metaphysical presence after I evacuate these reincarnations in brains of limited intelligence to pursue Wisdom. Gray, what do you suggest I do to get word to my next reiteration? I want to inform it to find out 'Who I am,' and what task I am supposed to do."

~ I'm starting to catch your drift, whichever way it happens to be going, Glish. If you're part of something bigger than humanity, you might want to paint a bigger picture than that image of time. Try to portray a creature who views one thousand earth–years all at one time. It's watching Ricky Nelson sing at a garden party right now. ~

"Excuse me, Gray, while I slide out of the way and glide over to the window where the Light is brighter."

~ Since my wife isn't here with me, I better not use the pronoun 'we' when the Examiner arrives or he I might appear dissociated. ~

"Think nothing of it. My Meta Muse associates and dissociates 'persons' long before the idea of Time commences. Hush, here it comes; I must vacate my premises."

~ What do I do while you're gone?" Sit here like an unconscious thing pondering a grand idea for the meaning of life? ~

"Ponder my next assignment, Gray. The physical part of 'us' must learn how to play that game. I weary of habitually playing the same trick on my carnal creature—making it forget I exist. The Muse of Ignorance loves what it does for his self esteem. I may reiterate as a toddler born to working class folks in Tangiers. Or, perhaps, I spiral upward to live in a sprightly Sun Demon spawned here on the earth. Perhaps I occupy a machine thriving in dry, dusty, cold, thin Martian air. If my next iteration unfolds with no matter at all, I am still first person singular. Take a moment; imagine me there."

~ Glish, I see a topical tale about time and life. Life is like a colossal jig–saw puzzle on loan to us. We borrow just enough of the other concept to put the puzzle together one moment at a time. ~

"And we do not even have a picture to show us how the project is supposed to look in the end."

Muse of the Meta Language here now; a word please. Silence! That goes for you too, N. Glish. Keep your thoughts to yourself. Nice work by the way; take the rest of the day off.

As for you, Brain, as boss of your Master or Mistress Muse, let me put this in words you can understand. Thanks to a Language you know, you are acquainted with the person, place, thing or noun you call Time, but you have no idea what you are thinking about.

The word has no taste, smell, tactile or audible features and no figure. That does not matter; the Native tongue gray cells are familiar with has little of importance to say. The Medium with the Message is the Muse of Life. Humans narrowly define it as biological in kind since much of what you find is material. However, the Language you know is, in and of itself, ethereal. Time is relevant to Life in a Language with a point of view one grade above nothing. It fills the emptiness with large amounts of stuffing. This makes Life in lower grades seem a smidgen more sensible until the Time comes to repay the loan, move up a grade and know Life is less meaningless and more comprehensible.

Always remember, Thingamajig, we examine, not experience of empirical evidence, but expressions employing words. Thus we explore, not sensational existence, but expositions explaining the eternal Medium of Life.

Enough of that for now, Brain. Your task, should you decide to accept it before you self destruct, as Mother Nature lawfully compels you to do, is to compare and contrast the concept of Time to Eternity. You have from now until the moment when the moron by the window wakes to go to work.

Begin.

www.ingramcontent.com/pod-product-compliance
Lightning Source LLC
LaVergne TN
LVHW010614100826
845148LV00014B/2957

* 9 7 8 1 7 3 5 4 4 8 3 2 9 *